CHARLIE AND THE GRANDMOTHERS

ALSO BY KATY TOWELL

Skary Childrin and the Carousel of Sorrow

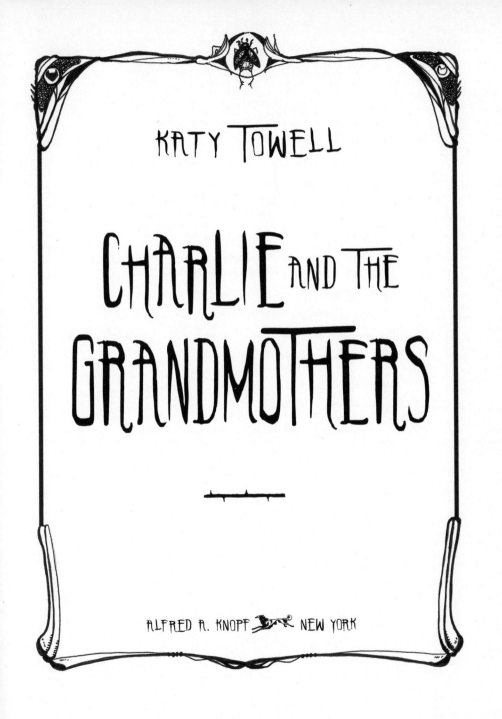

KATY TOWELL

CHARLIE AND THE GRANDMOTHERS

ALFRED A. KNOPF · NEW YORK

THIS IS A BORZOI BOOK PUBLISHED BY ALFRED A. KNOPF

Visit us on the Web! randomhousekids.com

Educators and librarians, for a variety of teaching tools, visit us at RHTeachersLibrarians.com

Library of Congress Cataloging-in-Publication Data
Towell, Katy.
Charlie and the grandmothers / Katy Towell.—First edition.
p. cm.
Summary: When fearful twelve-year-old Charlie and his bolder younger sister are sent to visit a grandmother they never knew they had, they discover a dark secret.
ISBN 978-0-375-86860-3 (trade) — ISBN 978-0-375-96859-4 (lib. bdg.) — ISBN 978-0-375-89932-4 (ebook)
[1. Brothers and sisters—Fiction. 2. Grandmothers—Fiction. 3. Supernatural—Fiction. 4. Fear—Fiction. 5. Horror stories.] I. Title.
PZ7.T6488Ch 2015
[Fic]—dc23
2014038891

The text of this book is set in 12.5-point Adobe Jenson.
The illustrations were created using pen and ink.

Printed in the United States of America
August 2015
10 9 8 7 6 5 4 3 2 1

First Edition

This book is for my Grandmother Muriel,
who wanted you all to know that
she has a garden hoe filed into a hook.

This book is also for my Grandma Betty,
who, if she were still with us,
would have read this book
and said with a giggle,
"Well, bless your little heart."

CONTENTS

Chapter One: Charlie and Georgie 1

Chapter Two: Rag and Bone 17

Chapter Three: The Wrong Room 40

Chapter Four: The Old Tree 57

Chapter Five: Behind the Little Door 77

Chapter Six: The Stuff of Nightmares 95

Chapter Seven: Pigeon 116

Chapter Eight: The Queen 138

Chapter Nine: The Phantoms 158

Chapter Ten: Spoons and Hammers 173

Chapter Eleven: The Worst Memory 192

Chapter Twelve: An Alarming Turn of Events 205

Chapter Thirteen: Charlie and Georgie and Mother 215

CHAPTER ONE

CHARLIE AND GEORGIE

Charlie was awake.

Charlie was *always* awake if he could possibly help it. He hadn't slept properly in over six years. Not since that snowy February night when his slumber was broken by a pounding on the front door of the house, and a tall, sad man with his hat in his hands told Mother that an accident at the mill had taken Father away forever. Now when Charlie slept, he had bad dreams, and he would wake from these dreams with a terrible start, frightened that some new awfulness might've happened while his eyes were closed.

But it wasn't a nightmare that troubled Charlie this night. What troubled him now was as real as the dark circles under his eyes. He'd been warning of it for some time, but of course nobody ever listened.

It was the children. All the children in town were disappearing, and Charlie knew that his sister and he were next.

*   *   *

In fairness to everyone who never heeded his warnings, it's important to know that Charlie Oughtt was an exceptionally nervous twelve-year-old boy. He worried about flooding on a cloudless day. He worried about wildfires when the rain wouldn't stop. He worried about things that went bump in the night and worried equally about things that didn't. Charlie worried about everything all the time, and any attempt to reason with him only made him suspect your motives.

Charlie's nervousness grew with him until it wrote itself upon his paper-pale face as plainly as the text in the books he was always reading. He wore two inverted parentheses between his eyebrows at all times, and there were commas at the corners of his perpetually downturned mouth. One curl of his short brown hair stood up on the back of his head like a question mark, and he bore a hyphen-shaped scar where he habitually bit into his bottom lip.

"Squirrelly Charlie," his schoolmates called him, and sometimes "Oughtt the Distraught." "Young Charlie is a well-mannered student who excels in every subject," a teacher once wrote, "particularly in gym class, where he performs expertly as a hurdle."

Mother often said to herself that she wished Charlie were just a little bit more like his sister, to which she would invariably add, "and if only his sister were a little bit more like *him*." For Georgie Oughtt had never been afraid of anything in all her eight years. Rarely was there a day when she did not come home with a muddied frock or a scraped-up shin or with the landlady angrily pulling her along by the ear.

"Well, Georgie Louise, what have you to say for yourself this time?" was how Mother's lectures always began.

2

"I'm awfully sorry, Mama," Georgie would sweetly say, "but when adventure comes calling, how can an adventurer say no?" (Adventurers, she would then be reminded, sometimes needed to sit silently in their bedrooms for the rest of the day.)

Mother was very patient with her troubled worrier and her intrepid adventurer, for that is just the sort of person Mother was. Patient, kind, understanding. But Mother was also very sad. Sometimes she sighed for no reason that anyone could see, and often she fell very quiet. She almost always smiled, but it was a melancholy smile, and all the pretty jigs she taught her piano students sounded like elegies by the end of each lesson. Because Mother was so very lonely, it pained her to be away from her children for even a moment.

"I don't know how Mr. and Mrs. Thomas can bear to have their girls so far away!" she sighed when little Ellie and Margaret from Georgie's class went off to visit their grandmother one July.

"I'm sure it will be a wonderful time for the boy, but my heart aches for his mother," she said when one of her students left for a trip to see his grandmother the following August.

"It doesn't make you unhappy to see your friends travel when you're stuck here with me, does it?" she asked Georgie when the children from three doors down went to visit *their* grandmother in September.

"Not as unhappy as it would make me to leave you," Georgie answered, though this had only been half true.

"I don't want to travel anywhere, Mother," Charlie said, which was true as true could be. "We might be overtaken by train robbers, and who would take care of you then?"

Their answers made Mother smile in her sad way, especially when the twins from upstairs left in October.

"They're going away to visit their grandmother, aren't they?" Charlie asked as he watched them board a coach in the pouring rain. Mother didn't answer right away. Instead, she stopped playing her woeful tune and peered at Charlie from over the piano.

"You've got that tone in your voice," she said.

"They are, aren't they?" Charlie returned. "They always do."

"The twins?"

"All the children. They've all been going away, and they always have the same reason. It's . . . it's . . . it's odd is what it is."

"What's so odd about it?" Georgie asked as she prepared a poultice for her latest run-in with poison oak. "Lots of children go to visit their grandparents. I'm sure we would do the same if we had any left, and if you weren't afraid the sky would fall on us."

Mother resumed her playing and tsked at Georgie's manners at the same time. There was the usual be-nice-to-your-brother-Georgie-Louise and the typical but-she's-right-you-know-Charlie, and so Charlie kept his concerns to himself for a time. Meanwhile, the other children continued going away, one after another, even in the first blizzard of January.

"It just isn't normal," Charlie insisted one day, his nose pressed to the parlor window, his breath making the glass fog. "Their parents aren't even waving goodbye."

"It is a bit unusual," Georgie agreed, tracing a skull and crossbones in the foggy spot with her finger, "but if it's not a trip to see their grandmother, what else do you suppose it is? I've seen a lot in

4

my time, you know. I've been to every corner of our block. Often enough, Charlie-O, things are exactly what they appear to be. No matter how much I'd like for them to be a treasure map, sometimes they're just an advertisement that's bled through a wet newspaper."

"I really wish you wouldn't go digging up soggy garbage, Georgie. Think of all the mold spores you're breathing in," Charlie warned. Once, he'd read an article about a man who'd been the picture of health until his house flooded and subsequently mildewed. When the man took ill and died, the doctors opened up his head to find his brain as moldy as old cheese. It was weeks before Charlie would go near anything damp without holding his breath.

But Charlie wasn't really thinking about mold now. He was thinking that of all the children who had gone away since July, not one of them had come back. And no one but he seemed to mind. *At least Georgie and I are safe,* he thought. *Mother would never send us away. She needs us here.*

Then February came, and a colder, darker February Charlie could not recall. He already loathed the month as it was. His worst dreams plagued him relentlessly on the snowy nights of February. And now the sun had begun to disappear as early as noon while the snow fell so heavily that one had to bat the stuff out of the way in order to see where one was going. As usual, nobody found this as alarming as Charlie did.

"The days are always shorter in winter," reasoned Mother.

"All this gorgeous snow and not one friend around to throw a ball of it at," Georgie harrumphed.

Charlie shook his head impatiently after the umpteenth round of this and swore to himself he'd give up while wondering why he bothered at all. But he knew very well why he bothered. He bothered because he believed in every one of his bones that some evil lurked in those snowy black nights, and if he closed his eyes too long, it would come in and snatch away all that he loved. In truth, he had always felt so, but everyone told him not to let his imagination run away with him. Now that the night came so unnaturally early, and what with all the kids he knew drifting away, Charlie couldn't be satisfied that all his years of fearful expectation were the product of nervous fancy.

So, night after night he waited, hunched over his favorite encyclopedia volume with a mug of hot black coffee to keep him awake. Morning after morning, Mother would find him shivering under his blankets and would have to promise him that whatever threat he had perceived was now long gone with the morning sun.

But then came the darkest night of them all.

It was a distinct and almost tangible darkness that made the hair stand up on Charlie's neck. It jolted him from his reading and compelled him to peek through his curtains, where he saw, to his great alarm, nothing. No streetlamps, no wandering beam from the distant lighthouse. The moon had turned black, and while he watched, the very stars went out. Soon after, the noise he usually took for granted long into the night was silenced all at once. No carts rolling on cobblestones, no chatter from late-shift dockworkers, no seagulls screeching. It was as if some great awful being were cupping its hands over the world to snuff it out. Then Charlie's own lamp sputtered and died, leaving him in blackness with a thundering heart.

What if it's me? he thought. *What if I've gotten myself so frightened that all my senses are short-circuiting? Maybe everything is completely fine out there, and I've just gone deaf and blind. Oh dear. That isn't any better at all!*

Charlie's senses were not on the fritz, it turned out, a fact soon proved when he heard a voice coming from his mother's room next door. Charlie slipped out of bed and, after stumbling about in the darkness, found the wall and pressed his ear to it.

"Yes," he heard Mother murmur. "That . . . would be . . . lovely. Pearl. I . . . always . . . loved . . . that farm . . . of pearls. . . ."

Farm of pearls? She must be dreaming, Charlie thought. But then he heard a sound that made his breath catch in his throat. It was another voice. A strange, whispering voice only just audible to the sort of person who makes a practice of listening for strange voices.

"See the world, the worldy-worldy-world," it hissed in a childish way.

"They should . . . experience . . . the world. Shouldn't . . . keep them here . . . all the . . . time. . . ." Mother yawned.

"Sleep now. Sleepy-sleepy-sleep!"

"I . . . have been . . . so very tired. . . ."

"Happy! So happy! No need for kiddies!"

Charlie ran to the curtain that divided his half of the room from his sister's, slipping on the rug in the process. He scrambled to his feet again, ignoring the pain in his undoubtedly bruised knee, and hissed, "Georgie! Georgie, wake up! Someone's in Mother's room!"

He fumbled for the curtain and pulled it back. In the darkness so absolute, he couldn't see his sister, but there was no mistaking her snoring. Georgie could have slept through a hurricane, and trying to wake

7

her up always proved a waste of time. But there wasn't any time to waste, and Charlie knew he couldn't bury himself in his blankets now.

"Mother!" he shouted, and after much clattering and stumbling and knocking over of things, he made his way to their mother's room and threw open her door.

When he looked inside, however, he saw no one in the room but Mother. The terrible darkness had lifted. All was illuminated by the hazy glow of the moon now. Through the sheer curtains on Mother's window, the streetlamps kept their usual watch. Below, the fishmongers sang while they packed up their wares, just as they did every night. It seemed then as if all Charlie had witnessed before had happened days ago, his memory of it disintegrating like the horror of nightmares by morning.

"Charlie?" Mother mumbled groggily, half sitting. "What's going on? Are you all right? What's happened?"

"Nothing," Charlie said, feeling like a fool. "It was just a bad dream."

Nevertheless, when Charlie returned to his own room, he peeked out his window once more, just to be sure. He saw a policeman idly pacing the boardwalk. A seagull was decimating a crab. A stray cat perched atop a barrel and cleaned its paws. All under the flames of streetlamps that dotted the night's fog like ghost lights. Everything was as it should be.

And yet something caught Charlie's eye. Standing but a few yards from the apartment house was a very old woman in a dusty, tattered dress, her shaggy hair draping her hunched shoulders. She leaned on a wooden cart full of junk and was accompanied on either side by a pair of what Charlie supposed were small children, though their clothes and hats were so oversized that he couldn't see their faces. They could've been trained monkeys for all he knew.

Charlie was still puzzling over this when he noticed that the old woman was staring right at him. There could be no mistake about it. Their eyes met, and she grinned, showing teeth as gray as her hair. Charlie gasped and pulled his curtains closed.

It's just some old rag-and-bone woman, he told himself. *Isn't there anything in the world I'm not afraid of?*

Charlie lay awake the rest of the seemingly ordinary night, staring at the utterly average ceiling until the unremarkable sun rose in the morning and shone plainly through the perfectly normal window. His weariness made his head feel like a strongman's barbell, but that wasn't anything out of the usual for him. Nor, for that matter, was the embarrassment from having panicked over nothing yet again.

Perhaps everybody's right about me, he thought. *At least the boy who cried wolf knew when he was making it all up.*

He reached out and took his alarm clock from his night table and examined its off-white face. The time was six-fifty-nine, and in exactly thirty-four seconds, the copper bells on top would start clanging away. Charlie never needed the alarm to wake up. He just liked that it was something he could count on every single day, without any surprises at all, as long as he remembered to wind it. Whenever Charlie felt as rotten as he did now, he looked to his alarm clock, and then everything seemed all right again.

But not everything was all right, for drifting from the kitchen was the sound of Mother humming. Not just humming, he noted with concern, but humming *happily*. Charlie sat up slowly, all his bones popping and cracking the way one's grandfather's might. Then he depressed the button that would quiet his beloved alarm clock before it rang unnecessarily and went to investigate this mystery of Mother's good cheer.

"Good morning, dear!" Mother sang when he entered. She was vigorously stirring something in a large bowl. Behind her, a fire roared dangerously within the stove, the door of which was wide open.

"What are you staring at, Charlie?" Mother asked with a wink. "Put one more log in, would you? I've got another batch of pancakes to put on."

"I—I don't . . . the f-f-fire . . . ," Charlie stammered.

"I'll do it, Mama," said Georgie from behind him.

Charlie started to advise his sister otherwise, but she put a finger to her lips, waited for Mother to turn her back, and then closed the stove door without another log.

"Thank you, darling!" said Mother, still stirring. "Now, if you'll both sit at the table, I'll have breakfast ready shortly."

"*What's going on?*" Charlie mouthed as he sat.

Georgie shrugged, wide-eyed. In the middle of the table, there were already three platters piled high with fluffy golden pancakes— far more than the children could eat even if it were all they ate for a week.

"Are you feeling all right, Mother?" Charlie asked.

Mother didn't seem to hear him and continued humming and stirring even more batter. She had begun to pour the next round into the pan on the stove when Charlie cleared his throat and said a little louder, "I think we already have more than we can eat, Mother. Why don't you sit down with us?"

"Well! If you're quite sure that's enough," said Mother, smiling with absurd exuberance. She carefully placed the bowl in the basin and wiped her hands right on her dress, apparently having forgotten an apron. Georgie giggled, for which Charlie gently kicked her under the table and shook his head.

"While you two are enjoying your breakfast," Mother said as she began serving pancakes onto the children's plates, "I have some marvelous news for you! I've received the most wonderful letter from your Grandmother Pearl!"

"From whom?" asked Charlie.

"Why, your Grandmother Pearl!" Mother repeated, still dishing out the cakes. "She has invited you both to spend the rest of the winter with her on her farm in the country! Isn't that perfect? I think it's perfect!"

Charlie choked without having even taken a bite. "What?" he sputtered.

"We have a Grandmother Pearl?" asked Georgie.

"Wh-what?" Charlie blurted again.

"Oh yes, children! She's missed you so. Why haven't I taken you to visit more often? I can't remember anymore. But no matter. It's just ever so perfect!" Mother sighed. The pile of pancakes on Charlie's plate had begun to lean now, but she did not seem to notice.

"You must leave quite soon, of course. It would be rude to keep her waiting when she's been so lovely to invite you. I'll help you pack, though you really won't need much—"

"Mother . . . *Mother!* That's enough for me, thank you," Charlie said, gently pushing away Mother's flapjack-laden spatula.

"But you love pancakes," said Mother in a faraway voice. "All children love pancakes."

Charlie and Georgie glanced at one another.

"Of course we do, Mama," Georgie said politely, "but remember that we're children, not elephants."

"Yes," said Mother, staring at the table. "I do forget sometimes."

Georgie gave Charlie a worried look, but he motioned for her to say nothing.

"Speaking of forgetting," he said to Mother, "I don't think we remember a Grandmother Pearl. I thought both of our grandmothers had passed away some time ago."

Charlie did not merely *think* that their grandmothers had passed away. He was certain of it, for he clearly recalled attending each of their funerals. And while he did not remember either of the ladies terribly well, he did remember how everybody present had looked like shadows in their mourning attire and how frightened he had been of the statues in the graveyard with their blank faces.

"Why, whatever is the matter with you, Charlie?" chided Mother. "Grandmother Pearl is your *grandmother!* She has that lovely farm! You remember, don't you? That lovely farm of Pearl's?"

At once, Charlie felt his flesh crawl. He didn't remember any grandmother named Pearl, but he most certainly did remember the mysterious voice he had heard only just last night. He had thought it all a dream, but now he wasn't so sure. "I always loved that farm of pearls," Mother had said to someone. Charlie had misheard it at the time, but now he understood perfectly. That is, he understood enough to be sure some foul plot was in the works.

"Mama," said Georgie, "why don't you tell us about this farm? Seeing as Charlie and I can't remember it."

"Well, you know . . . ," said Mother, and it was several seconds before she had collected her thoughts. "It's very green with lots of things growing. And there are horses grazing, and cows lowing, and a nanny goat who wears a bell about her neck. It's ever so perfect. You'll be very happy there."

But even as Mother described this perfect picture of a place, it seemed to Charlie that she was simply trying to remember what a farm even was. She spoke as if in a fog, and her gaze was as empty as their pantry now was of flour. Charlie could not imagine what had come over Mother, but he was sure that if she were in her right mind, she would never send his sister and him away at all, let alone to a grandmother they had never known. Certainly not when so many other children had gone missing for similar reasons! Had their parents lost their minds as well? Was this why no one cared if they never returned?

"We're not going," he said quietly.

"What?" said Mother.

"I'm sorry, Mother, but we're not going to see Grandmother Pearl," said Charlie.

"But why?" Mother asked.

Georgie glanced back and forth between her mother and her brother and sank down in her seat.

"Because you're not yourself right now, and we don't know anybody named Pearl, and I think . . . well, I think . . ." Charlie struggled to reason. "I think you've taken ill, and we're not going to leave you here like that. Absolutely not."

Mother gasped and stood, though Charlie noticed she was a bit unsteady on her feet.

"I-I-I've never heard such disrespect!" she exclaimed. "Such disobedience! Such disregard! Such—"

"Might I be excused?" Georgie sheepishly asked, only to be ignored.

"Such distasteful behavior!" Mother went on.

"Mother, please listen," Charlie pleaded, but Mother was quite beside herself.

"Go to your room this minute!" she shouted.

"But, Mama, he's only—" Georgie protested.

"You as well, Georgie Louise! Not another word!" Mother insisted. "Grandmother Pearl loves you both very much, and it was very kind of her to send for you! You will spend the rest of the morning in your room without breakfast. Perhaps it will help you remember your manners when your stomachs are all a-rumble at school!"

Charlie and Georgie gaped at one another. This was not like Mother at all. She *never* shouted. The closest either Charlie or Georgie had seen their mother come to it was when Georgie tricked Charlie into believing he'd come down with "deadly pirate's influenza," and even then, Mother had only very sternly said she was disappointed.

"Don't be sad, Charlie," Georgie said once they returned to their room. "I've decided that Mama's just behaving this way so that we'll *want* to leave. It must be very hard for her to part with us."

"But why is she trying to send us away at all?" Charlie asked.

"She said there was a letter from Grandmother Pearl—" Georgie began.

"But who *is* Grandmother Pearl? What if she doesn't really exist?" said Charlie. "Don't you see? Mother could be trying to ship us off to someplace terrible. Someplace we might never come back from just like everyone else! Last night I heard her talking to someone in her sleep. I thought I imagined it, but after this morning, it all makes sense. She's been hypnotized!"

"Hypnotized by whom? A wicked wizard?" Georgie laughed.

Charlie shook his head and sat down on his bed, drawing his knees up to his chest.

Georgie sat down beside him. "You've just been thinking too much," she said. "I'd bet all the other children who went away had a fine time with their grandmothers. And then their grandmothers each wrote to all the other grandmothers they knew and said, 'I had a fine time with my grandchildren. You ought to invite yours over to stay, too!' and then it became the fashionable thing to do."

"But we don't *have* a Grandmother Pearl!" Charlie insisted.

"Maybe we've just forgotten we do," suggested Georgie, and Charlie threw himself back on the bed with a groan.

CHAPTER TWO

RAG AND BONE

Charlie was lost in the direst of thoughts that morning as he walked Georgie to her schoolhouse and then trudged onward to his own. He wondered about the change that had come over Mother. One moment she was as foggy as could be, and the next she was scarlet with anger. And all over a most perplexing mystery. *Could illness be the reason?* he pondered. *Could it be that all the parents in town were ill, and this sending off of children was but a symptom of a contagious brain fever?* It was a frightening thought, but so was the idea of traveling to the unknown. Why did anyone ever want to see new places anyway? Why couldn't everyone be as happy to sit safely at home and read encyclopedias as he was?

But Charlie's gloom would be temporarily disrupted, for among the strangers he saw on his walk was a familiar figure in a dingy old dress. Beside her were the same two urchins swaddled in too-large clothing.

"Rag and bo-oooone! Rag and bo-oooone! Anything will do!" sang the old woman as Charlie hurried to pass her. He could feel her eyes burning into him, but he dared not look back. Those eyes had seemed so empty when he saw them last. Empty and yet full with purpose at the same time. *Stop thinking like that!* he scolded himself.

"Give us what ye don't want! Trade for something new!" the woman called after him. He knew that her cries were for anyone with goods to trade, but he couldn't help but feel like she had taken special interest in him. *Or maybe I'm just afraid of the elderly along with everything else.* Still, he couldn't be sure it was only his imagination when he heard one of the urchins hiss at him as he moved by.

School that day was an awful chore to get through, even though the loathsome gym class was canceled due to the snow. Charlie simply couldn't focus on a single lesson. It was no help at all that his classes were so sparsely attended. *They're all with their grandmothers,* Charlie thought of his absent classmates. *Or wherever their parents really sent them.*

"I do hope Mama's not upset with us anymore," said Georgie when Charlie met her at the end of the school day.

"Me too, Georgie," said Charlie. "Me too."

But they would never know how Mother felt about them, for she was asleep in bed when they returned. She even slept through dinnertime, and Charlie had to make cheese sandwiches for his sister and himself. Mother slept through the night as well, though Charlie did not, and she was still asleep when morning came.

"Do you think we ought to wake her?" whispered Georgie as the children stood over her that evening, watching.

"I've already tried," said Charlie.

In fact, he had tried everything in the book, but no amount of nudging or prodding or shaking or calling Mother's name would rouse her. She muttered strange things in her sleep, and sometimes she rolled over on her side, but she would not wake. Not for a moment. Even Georgie was troubled now.

When yet another morning came without any change, Charlie decided to take action.

"Dr. Kenneth will know what to do," he told Georgie as he put on his coat and cap.

"He's always patched us up when we're broken, hasn't he?" said Georgie as she felt Mother's forehead for fever.

"Always," said Charlie. He walked calmly out of the house so as not to reveal his panic to his sister. But once he was outdoors, he sprinted down the street as fast as he could manage without slipping on the scattered patches of ice. He was perfectly aware that it might have been faster to call a cab, but he wasn't sure he knew how to do it. Nor was he certain that the driver would not be a bank robber in disguise or that the horses wouldn't get spooked by something and run away while Charlie sat helplessly in the carriage. So, he remained on foot, running past the fish market and trying not to breathe in the smell. Running into bystanders half a dozen times, for which they shouted at him and shook their fists. Running as if he had fire at his heels. All the while, it snowed as if the sky were falling apart at the seams, and the snow seeped through his boots, freezing his toes until they ached horribly.

At last he reached the neat little row of houses that included Dr. Kenneth's home and office. His was the town house in the very center—a tidy building of violet bricks with turquoise frames around its three stories of windows and doors. It was the brightest house of the lot. All the others were probably stately white affairs once, but now they were the same gray that matched nearly everything else by the docks. Only Dr. Kenneth's house managed to retain its cheeriness, which seemed to reflect the doctor's own personality. But today even his house looked a tad grim, for which Charlie credited the miserable weather.

When Charlie stepped inside, he saw something more troubling than gray skies and blustering snow. The waiting room was unusually empty, for one thing. For another, Dr. Kenneth's secretary, Miss Markham, was absent. In her place at the front desk was the doctor himself. An ordinary person might see this as a blessing. An average individual who hadn't noticed the strange goings-on of late might say to himself, "How fine. There won't be a wait today," but Charlie wasn't that sort of person. This was all very much out of the ordinary, and it stank of ill fortune.

"How can I help you?" said Dr. Kenneth without looking up. He was thumbing through Miss Markham's appointment book, though he didn't appear to be reading any of it.

"I'm . . . I'm here to see you, sir," said Charlie, removing his cap.

Dr. Kenneth yawned and flipped another page of the book. "Yes, that is obvious," he said blandly, "but what is it that you *need?*"

Charlie didn't care for the doctor's tone of voice. Dr. Kenneth was normally quite kind. He was certainly patient, given how often he'd treated Georgie for the very same injuries over the very same calamities without once chiding her. What in the world could be the explanation for such coldness now? And where was Miss Markham? Her absence bothered Charlie every bit as much as Dr. Kenneth's indifference. Nevertheless, Charlie told the man his troubles.

"If you could go and see Mother, I'm sure you would know what to do," he concluded.

But Dr. Kenneth only looked at him with dull eyes and a weary smile before he said, "I'm afraid I'm all booked up for the next month. If you'd like to leave a request for an appointment, I'll be sure to see you as soon as my time is free."

"A month?!" Charlie squeaked. "But it'll be too late by then! I'm sure of it!"

"My hands are full," explained the doctor. "With Miss Markham away on holiday, my time is quite taken up."

Charlie's mouth fell open. All he could do was stand there like a fool. But then Dr. Kenneth blinked a few times and brightened.

"You say your mother is sleeping a lot?" he asked.

"Y-yes, sir," said Charlie.

"And is this not a typical habit of hers?"

"No, sir. No, she doesn't usually even nap."

Dr. Kenneth clasped his hands together. "There, you see?" he said. "It's quite simple. Your mother has worn herself out from looking after you, and she's catching up on much-needed sleep. I'm sure that if you give her the peace she deserves, she'll wake up as good as new, and you'll see that everything is perfectly fine. Perfectly, perfectly fine."

"You don't understand, sir," Charlie insisted. "She's not herself. She—"

"Perfectly fine," the doctor repeated, more to himself than to Charlie. He had now gone back to staring blankly at the appointment book.

Meanwhile, Charlie's patience was growing very thin. Dr. Kenneth wasn't simply unfeeling. His head appeared to be in the clouds. Perhaps even the same clouds that had descended upon Mother before the sleep came over her. There was a strangely familiar tinge to the doctor's odd behavior.

"Is there anyone else who could come see my mother?" Charlie asked through clenched teeth. "Anyone at all?"

"If you really feel you must see a doctor, there is a fine physician on the west side of town," Dr. Kenneth suggested with a lazy wave of his hand, "but his fees are perhaps too much for you."

"H-how much does he charge?" Charlie asked.

"More than a family living on *this* side of town can afford," the doctor answered with another yawn. "Good day, young man. My best wishes to your mother." Then he went back to the appointment book, staring at it with glazed eyes and probably not a care in the world for anyone listed within it.

Charlie was stunned. He was speechless. Why, he was *furious* and felt the doctor should be ashamed of himself! But Charlie did not have the courage to say so out loud; he wasn't sure what good it would do anyway. Instead, he politely thanked Dr. Kenneth and then returned to the street in a shroud of hopelessness. So heavy was this hopelessness that Charlie could walk only so far before he found he needed to sit and unload the burden of his thoughts.

What am I going to do? he thought. The Oughtt family was never hungry, but they certainly hadn't any money to spare. Charlie considered finding work, but what work there was for boys his age didn't pay well; he was sure of it. Neither was it likely to pay quickly enough. He supposed he could try and plead with this other doctor, but he hadn't much hope. Charlie's chances of getting any help at all seemed as weak as tea from thrice-brewed leaves.

It was during this moment of dejection that Charlie heard a squeaking sound. *Scree! Scree! Scree!* it went—the creaking of cart wheels quite close by. The hair stood up on the back of his neck; he had a feeling he knew whose cart it was. And he was right, for there, not two feet from him, stood the rag-and-bone woman. She grinned at him with her mouthful of stained teeth, watching him with a direct stare that had no soul behind it. To Charlie's relief, she was unaccompanied by the urchins, at least. All she had with her now was her cart full of junk.

"H-hello," said Charlie, for he wasn't sure what else to do.

"What's your name, boy?" the old woman asked him in a thin, warbling voice. It was the sort of voice he imagined witches to have.

"Charlie," he said in a cautious tone, and he slowly rose to his feet.

"What-what-what?" said the woman, putting a gnarled, spotty hand to her ear and rolling her pale eyes to the sky. "Charlie *what?*"

"I'm sorry, ma'am," said Charlie, "but I'm afraid I don't know you well enough to—"

"You do *remember* all your names, don'tcha?" the woman interrupted him.

"Of course I do. It's just that I'd rather not—" Charlie began, but she interrupted him yet again.

"*Always hold on to your names!*" she hissed. She looked all about

24

herself, her eyes darting this way and that. Then she tapped her head and said, "Keep 'em safe up here."

"Er, yes, thank you. I will," Charlie replied with a polite smile, then he tipped his cap and made to slip past her when suddenly she said, "Your mama's got sick, ain't she?"

Charlie stopped and turned back. "How do you know about my mother?" he asked.

The old woman giggled and drummed her grimy fingers together. She was so dirty it was hard to tell where her glovelettes ended and her fingers began. "The buggies march in two by two," she sang, bouncing on her toes, "and they make little puppets o' me and you!"

She's completely bonkers, Charlie thought. He felt bad for the old peddler, but she frightened him a very great deal. How *did* she know about Mother? Had she followed him? Charlie reached into his pocket for his house key and slowly removed it, gripping it tightly. His plan was to run home and let himself inside as quickly as possible. But then the old woman shrieked, and he was so shocked he couldn't move.

"The key!" she screeched, and she lunged for him, snatching the key right out of his hand.

"Hey!" Charlie shouted. "Give that back!"

But then the peddler woman inspected the key, turned it over twice, and stuck her tongue out in disgust.

"*That's* not the key," she harrumphed, and flung it to the ground. She said, "I had the key, but it ran away when I gave my names to the two-faced queen."

"The . . . two-faced queen?" said Charlie. He knelt slowly to pick up his key, keeping a close watch on the old woman as he did.

"Aye," she said. Then, "Ah!" and she rummaged through her cart until she had extracted a bedraggled china doll. It had no hair, the ugly thing, and its eyes were missing from its sockets.

"Here," said the woman, tapping a long yellow fingernail on the doll's chest. "That's where it goes."

"I see. Thank you for the information. I had better be going now," Charlie said with a nervous smile, but before he even realized what was happening, the old woman tossed the doll into his arms. He stared at it in surprise, unsure of what to do with it. Then a shiny black beetle emerged from one of the empty eyeholes.

"Oh gosh!" he gasped, and he dropped the doll at once.

"Oh. Gosh," he said again, for a long crack had now formed from the top of the doll's porcelain head down to where its cotton body began. He started to apologize, but when he looked up, he saw that the woman was staring over her shoulder and wringing her hands. A short distance behind her, the two urchins were making their way over. To tell the truth, they made him even more uncomfortable than the rag-and-bone woman. They looked like goblins, with their features all covered up in oversized clothes. Perhaps they were goblins, Charlie thought, for the rag-and-bone woman had begun fretting awfully.

"Oh, I've been bad again," she was saying, paying no attention to the doll in the dirt. "Eyes and ears. Ears and eyes. That's all I'm meant to be. Best get back to it before them sandies hear. But I don't like to. I don't like to." At last, she shuffled away, still muttering to herself over the *scree-scree-scree* of her cart wheels.

Charlie gave a great sigh of relief. He'd have quite a story to tell

Georgie once home, but the first thing he planned to do when he got there was give his hands a good scrubbing. When he arrived, however, Georgie was waiting at the door.

"Charlie! Charlie! A telegram's come!" she exclaimed. "It's from Grandmother Pearl! She says she'll help Mama!"

"Georgie!" Charlie halfheartedly scolded. "You know what Mother says about reading her letters."

"But it's addressed to us!" said Georgie.

Charlie snatched the piece of paper from his sister's hand and read. It said:

```
DEAREST CHARLIE AND GEORGIE=

WORD HAS REACHED ME OF YOUR MOTHERS ILLNESS=
I UNDERSTAND SHE IS IN NEED OF URGENT CARE=
I WILL ARRANGE TO HAVE HER TAKEN TO AN EXCELLENT
HOSPITAL ON CONDITION THAT YOU BOTH COME TO ME AT
ONCE=
IT WOULD NOT DO FOR YOU TO BE ALONE WITHOUT
SOMEONE TO LOOK AFTER YOU=
A COACH WILL ARRIVE IN THE MORNING TO TAKE YOU TO
THE TRAIN STATION=
A PROPER DOCTOR WILL COME TO FETCH YOUR MOTHER
SOON AFTER=
ALL HAS BEEN ARRANGED=

WITH LOVE ALWAYS=

YOUR GRANDMOTHER PEARL.
```

"There, you see? I knew she was good!" said Georgie.

Charlie shook his head.

"No?!" said Georgie.

"No," said Charlie. "It's too suspicious. How do you suppose she found out about Mother's illness? How could word have possibly reached her that fast?"

"Maybe Mama sent her a telegram like this one," offered Georgie.

"But when?" asked Charlie. "I'm telling you, it doesn't smell right."

Georgie groaned and plodded into the parlor, flopping down onto Mother's piano bench. "What did Dr. Kenneth say?" she asked, angrily hammering an off-key rendition of "Mary Had a Little Lamb" with one finger.

"He seemed to think Mother's condition was perfectly normal," Charlie said, "but to tell you the truth, I'm not sure we can count on Dr. Kenneth right now. There is another doctor, only I don't think we have the money."

"Then what else are we to do, Charlie?" Georgie asked. "We *must* go to Grandmother Pearl!"

"It's not as simple as that," said Charlie.

But she's right, he thought. What choice did they have? Mother needed help, and there wasn't a single thing he could think of to do. Now this Grandmother Pearl, whoever she might be, was offering to take care of everything if only they would go and see her. He wasn't sure how she could have known. Perhaps news really did travel fast. Perhaps Mother had written to her after all. Or perhaps the idea that a stranger would arrange all of this just to do them harm was even more absurd than an unfamiliar grandmother asking them to visit.

"I need a minute to think," he said. Then he walked back to Mother's room and stood beside her bed as she slept, pale as a ghost.

He gave her hand a squeeze, but she did not respond. Yes, a decision would have to be made, and only Charlie could make it. Despite all his misgivings, he knew what that decision would have to be. There simply wasn't time for anything else.

"I'm afraid we're going to have to leave you, Mother," Charlie said softly. "So, please get better quickly. Before morning if you can. Because I don't know what's going to happen to us when we go."

All that night, Charlie huddled in the back corner of his bed, gazing off at nothing in particular like a condemned prisoner resigned to his fate. Not even his alarm clock could bring him comfort now. *I should run away*, he thought. *I should take Georgie and run away once we're dropped off at the station. She'd probably come along; it would be one of those adventures she likes so much. We could come back to make sure Mother's been fetched off to the hospital, and it would be at least a day before Grandmother Pearl found out she'd been double-crossed. Then we'd hide until Mother wakes up, and she* has *to wake up eventually. She* has *to.*

But Charlie knew they would never really run. He was too afraid.

No, the Oughtt children did not run away. When the sun rose upon their traveling day, the coach driver found them wide-awake and waiting—one with excitement and worry, the other with only worry.

"I bet there will be warm cookies waiting for us," Georgie rambled as she tightened her bootlaces, "and pines all covered in snow like Christmas trees!"

"Or suspicious men in waxed mustachios," Charlie grumbled as he helped his sister with her coat, "waiting to kidnap us and sell us to a traveling circus."

Charlie could only hope that the spell upon Mother would break soon, and she would stop all this nonsense before Georgie and he were out the door possibly forever. But nothing had changed by the time the children's things were loaded onto the coach. Mother still slept, oblivious to the plight of her children.

Charlie took one last look at his neighborhood before leaving. The weather was calm. Their apartment house looked like it did every day. The townspeople busied themselves as usual—as if nothing terrible were happening right under their noses. *Because nobody sees what's going on here*, he thought sadly. *Nobody sees it but me.*

"It'll be all right, Charlie," said his sister beside him, patting his arm. "I'm sure Mother will write to us when she gets better, and we'll have so many wonderful stories to tell her that we'll have to send our replies with two stamps each!"

"I hope you're right," Charlie said with a sigh.

"Think of it as an adventure!" Georgie chirped.

But I hate adventures, Charlie thought. Then he closed the door, left his key under the mat for whoever was meant to fetch their mother, and followed Georgie down the front path to the waiting coach. Together, the Oughtt children left their home like all the other children had—with no one waving goodbye and no promise of ever returning.

*   *   *

Georgie asked all the questions after that. Charlie knew his questions could only have the worst possible answers, so he preferred not to ask anything at all.

"How will we know where to go when we get to the station? Will we have time to explore?" Georgie asked the coach driver.

"Everything's been arranged," he brusquely replied.

"How long will the trip be? Will they make us sit still the *whole* time?" Georgie later asked the stationmaster.

"It's all been arranged, young lady," was the stationmaster's tired response.

No matter what Georgie asked or of whom she asked it, the answer always came back the same. It had all been arranged. Charlie kept waiting for this arrangement to reveal some sinister mastermind with diabolical plans, but no such mastermind had shown himself thus far. If Charlie had learned anything from the true crime stories he used to read, however, it was that bad folk could reveal themselves anywhere and at any time. There was no weather forecast for evil in the newspaper.

So consumed by these thoughts was Charlie that he didn't notice they had already reached the train until he felt Georgie pulling him up the steps and into the car.

"Oh," he said once he realized. His stomach loop-de-looped. *It's begun*, he thought. *We're really leaving.*

"It's wonderful!" Georgie gushed over the train, though it was about as ordinary as any passenger car could be. There was a carpeted aisle down the center with rows of empty bench seats to the right and the left, each with its own little window. There were signs here and there, some with directions to other cars, some harshly reminding passengers of etiquette. There was nothing remarkable about any of it, really, but the last time they'd ridden a train had been after Father died, and Georgie had been too young then to remember it now.

"Oh, I wish Mama could be here to see this. Think of it, Charlie! We're traveling!" she squealed.

"There's no escaping now," Charlie said miserably.

Just then, a frail, bony hand landed upon his shoulder. Charlie yelped and spun around to find an elderly man in an official-looking hat grinning a bit too toothily for Charlie's comfort.

"Oh, ho ho! Didn't mean to scare you, young sir!" said the man in a thin, singsong voice. His eyes and the veins in his hands were the same pale blue. "I'm the conductor for this train. Mr. Topaz at your service! Now sit, kiddies, sit! For the train will soon depart!"

Charlie glanced around for suspicious passengers he should sit the farthest from. To his surprise, however, there was no one. No one at all.

"Are we the only riders?" he asked, but when he turned around, the conductor was already gone, and then Georgie was tugging him along by the arm again.

"Come on, Charlie! Let's *go*!" she urged.

"But there's no one else here! Doesn't that strike you as odd?" asked Charlie as he tried to keep up with his sister and avoid tripping over his shoelaces at the same time.

"It strikes *me* as having the whole car to ourselves," his sister answered as she plopped down upon a seat next to a window. She pressed her nose to the glass and grinned. "Look how far from home we are! Isn't it exciting? I can't even see our house from here!"

Charlie sat beside her and looked, but the view made him dizzy. He looked away quickly to find the conductor standing there, rubbing his veiny hands together almost greedily.

"All comfy-comfy-comfy?" he asked.

Something about the way he spoke unsettled Charlie deeply. Or perhaps it was the fact that he reminded him of the rag-and-bone lady with that awful grin and the same empty eyes. Then again, perhaps it was just the circumstance. Whatever the reason, the conductor gave him a terrible chill, and he recoiled, nodding quickly. Comfortable he most certainly was not, but he couldn't exactly divulge his theory that this entire journey was part of a larger plot to do away with the world's children.

"Good, good, good!" said the conductor with a giggle as he hobbled away. "Always happy to have new *children* aboard!"

As soon as the odd little man was out of earshot, Charlie turned to his sister again.

"Georgie, this is all making me very, very unhappy," he said through gritted teeth.

"I think Grandmother Pearl was very thoughtful to send for us," Georgie said. Charlie slumped, defeated.

The train blasted its whistle, steam clouded the station, and the scenery began to roll away. Soon, the station was behind them. City buildings became sparse. The trees grew dense. Charlie felt his chest tighten as all he knew fell behind them, but Georgie just babbled on and on about Grandmother Pearl and whatever Georgie supposed the farm to be like. It seemed she had already forgotten about their poor mother and forgot her all the more the farther they traveled from home.

Where are we going? Charlie thought. *Isn't anyone worried at all?*

He clutched his alarm clock tightly and stared helplessly at its face until the numbers began to blur. The *thump-bump* of the train over the tracks and Georgie's prattle soon softened and faded away. At last, Charlie's eyes closed against his will and he was lost to the sleep he'd denied himself the night before, suspended in dreams of winter's monsters.

A sweet and sickly smell crept under the cloak of Charlie's slumber and began dragging him back into consciousness. It was a cloying odor, like must and dying roses in rancid water. The smell of very old things.

As Charlie stirred, he became aware of a change in position. He was no longer vertical, and his back sank into something lumpier and stiffer than the plush train seats. What's more, he was utterly still. There was no rattling, no vibrations from the track. Only a strange, warm weight upon his chest. At last, the sleep-glue melted from Charlie's eyes, and he opened them to find himself fixed in the gaze of a very large, very fluffy white cat.

Charlie drew back, but the cat neither moved nor showed any surprise in its cold blue eyes. It was only when Charlie tried to sit up that the cat extended its claws, doing so just enough to keep its human perch in place.

Accepting defeat, Charlie kept still and took in his surroundings. He saw that he lay on a threadbare sofa the color of rotting plums. This sofa stood against the wall of a dim parlor cluttered with dusty bric-a-brac and furniture: a rocking chair with yarn and knitting needles, an upright piano that leaned to one side, a low mahogany table with a cobwebbed checkerboard in the center, shelves displaying glass figurines and wooden music boxes. Each wall of this room included an exit—two hallways on opposite sides, an opening that revealed a kitchen, and a weathered door flanked by two dirty windows.

Charlie had never, to his recollection, been to a grandmother's house before, but if ever there was a grandmotherly house, this was it. Yet if this *was* Grandmother Pearl's house, when had they arrived? Who had taken them from the train station to the house? Had he really slept through all that? And where was his sister?

"Georgie?" he called out.

From the direction of the kitchen, he heard the quick, light footsteps of his sister, accompanied by the much slower steps of someone he didn't know.

"He's awake! He's awake, Grandmothers!" he heard Georgie shout.

Grandmothers? Charlie thought. *Did she really say "grandmothers"? As in ... more than one?*

"You're awake!" Georgie announced again as she skidded into the room.

"Please help," said Charlie, pointing to the cat with the unwavering stare.

Not one but *two* elderly women entered then. One of them was very tall and thin. Her back bowed over dramatically, giving her the appearance of a windblown tree. She wore a faded black gown with a high collar of white lace. Silver hair lay balled up in a bun on the top of her head, and a cameo brooch decorated her reed-thin throat. She squinted at Charlie with red-rimmed eyes and did not smile.

The other one was short and plump with a similar dress made a little less stark by a lavender shawl draped about her shoulders. She kept her cloud-white hair wrapped around her head in a braid, and there were deep wrinkles around her eyes that made her look instantly cheerful. She peered at the children from over brass spectacles and smiled brightly.

"Oh, bless!" she said, and she hobbled closer to pluck the cat from Charlie's chest. Even at this, its gaze never left Charlie's face.

"How nice to find you awake, dear. I see you've already made friends with Talos!" said the shorter one as she deposited the cat on the floor. "I'm your Grandmother Opal."

"And I'm your Grandmother Pearl. Welcome," said the tall one. She smiled, too, but it appeared to pain her.

Charlie sat upright and smoothed the wrinkles out of his shirt. "Hello," he said warily. Then, "I don't think our mother mentioned you, Grandmother Opal."

"Everybody has a grandmother," said Grandmother Pearl in a distant voice. "One for every child."

Charlie didn't know what that was supposed to mean, but it gave him gooseflesh all the same. Grandmother Opal just shook her head and laughed. Her laughter had a pleasant and musical quality to it.

"Hush now, Grandmother Pearl! You'll make the boy nervous with all your strange talk!" she said. To Charlie, she explained, "We're sisters. But I would like for you to call me Grandmother Opal all the same. I never liked the word 'aunt.'"

"Yes, Grandmother Opal," Charlie said dutifully, if hesitantly. To tell it truly, he didn't feel particularly comfortable calling Grandmother Pearl his grandmother, either, but even in the depths of suspicion he always minded his manners.

"Do you know if our mother has been seen to?" he asked.

"You poor darlings," cooed Grandmother Opal. "Of course she has. Everything's been arranged, and you can be sure she'll be well looked after. How much of her do you remember?"

"Everything?" said Charlie, though he was baffled by the question. It seemed a curious thing to say to two children who had only just left home. What could they have possibly forgotten?

"Grandmother Pearl," said Grandmother Opal, clasping her hands together. Charlie noticed she wore a gold ring with a black gemstone as big as a knuckle. "Why don't we prepare the children's rooms for them?"

"Of course, Grandmother Opal," said Grandmother Pearl, her bare hands dead at her sides. "It is, after all, almost time."

"Time for what?" asked Georgie.

"Time for *bed*," the grandmothers answered in unison.

"But we've only just arrived!" Georgie complained. "Look, there's still a bit of sun out!"

She skipped to a window and pulled back the moth-eaten drapery. Charlie, now free of his furry jailer, stood and moved closer to see the sights. *Time to find out just where Mother would have sent us,* he thought as he approached the window.

But the sight he saw when he reached that window made the goose bumps on his arms sprout goose bumps of their own. This was no farm. This wasn't anything he expected at all. There were no animals. No trees save for a dead one that looked like a claw. Not a single piece of evidence that anything living existed here at all. Vanished was the ordinary if dour gray sky. In its stead was a rolling carpet of green clouds, darkening as the hidden sun began to set. And under the clouds stretched an icy wasteland as far as the eye could see.

CHAPTER THREE

THE WRONG ROOM

"What is this place?" Charlie croaked. He tried to swallow, but it seemed all the moisture in his throat had leaked out through his palms.

Outside, a frozen tumbleweed trundled across the icy plain.

"It's incredible," Georgie murmured.

Charlie shot his sister an appalled look. "But it's dead out there," he whispered. "It's dead, weird, and probably dangerous."

"I know!" Georgie said with a grin.

"Oh, but it's not dead at all, dear. Only dormant for the winter," said a voice from right behind the children.

Startled, Charlie jumped and then blushed. "Please excuse me, Grandmother Opal. I—I—I didn't mean to be rude," he stammered. "It's just that I've never been to a farm before, and I thought . . . Well, I thought—"

"You thought there would be fields full of cornstalks and horses galloping upon a grassy green?" Grandmother Opal finished for him with a chuckle. Charlie didn't answer.

"Not everything grows aboveground," Grandmother Pearl said from the kitchen doorway. "Not everything *we* grow."

Charlie knew very well that farms looked nothing in the winter like they did in the summer; it wasn't the lack of cornstalks and grassy green pasture that troubled him. The troubling thing for Charlie was how hard and empty the land appeared to be. *How could anything grow here*, he wondered, *regardless of the season?* Why, even in the city, during the harshest snows, there had always been some evidence of nature.

"Never fear, dear. I promise we'll erase all your worries soon," soothed Grandmother Opal. "Tomorrow over a nice, hot breakfast, your Grandmother Pearl and I will tell you everything you wish to know. You'd like that, wouldn't you?"

The children agreed, one more enthusiastically than the other.

"My, but you've had such a long journey, children, and here I am, keeping you both awake! How naughty of me!" Grandmother Opal said with a wink. "Of course, I would love to stay up chatting until the wee hours of the morning, but I'm afraid it's past our bedtimes as well. Grandmother Pearl and I are not so spry as we were at your age, dearies!"

"But we can keep up. When it is required of us," Grandmother Pearl added without warmth.

Georgie harrumphed. "All right," she conceded, though she cheered up again quickly, as was her way. After bidding her brother good-night, she skipped alongside Grandmother Opal down one of the two hallways.

"You'll love the room I've prepared for you, sweetest," Grandmother Opal was telling her as they disappeared into the shadows. "It's full of secret compartments and hidden openings. There's no telling what you might find tucked away in there!"

"Really? Could I get lost in there?"

"Possibly, darling. Quite possibly."

"Oh, Grandmother Opal, I can't wait to see it!"

She'll be all right, Charlie thought, though his twitching eye betrayed his anxiety. He really wanted to believe. Why shouldn't he? he wondered. Grandmother Opal seemed very nice so far, and Grandmother Pearl, though a touch odd, was too frail to really be dangerous. *Besides,* Charlie thought, *if they'd planned something horrible for us, it probably would've happened by now. Probably.*

Unless . . .

"Come along, Charlie. Your room is on the other side of the house," said Grandmother Pearl. Beside the old woman, Talos the cat stared.

Trying his best to ignore the grandmothers' feline familiar, Charlie followed Grandmother Pearl down the opposite hallway. An ornate purple pattern covered the walls here, occasionally revealing plaster where the faded damask had worn through. Cobwebs draped daguerreotypes that hung all in a row. These were portraits of families Charlie had never known. He tried to see if he recognized the grandmothers in any of them, but it was impossible to tell by only the dim light of Grandmother Pearl's candle, and the eyes of all the people pictured seemed to follow Charlie as he walked. He shuddered and kept his eyes on his feet. Sometimes, though, he caught a glimpse of Talos's small white paws beside him, and that made him shudder, too.

"How old is this house, Grandmother Pearl?" he asked.

"I suppose it's always been here," Grandmother Pearl answered without looking at him, "in one form or another."

Charlie wanted to ask what sort of answer that was and if Grandmother Pearl made a hobby of frightening her guests, but he decided to keep his thoughts to himself. At last, they reached a sharp turn in the hall, and here, before a dark door, they stopped.

"Welcome to your room, dear," Grandmother Pearl said, smiling in her forced way. She turned the tarnished brass handle, and the door opened with a horrendous groan.

But more horrible than the groan was the way Talos immediately arched his back and hissed at something Charlie couldn't see. He would see it soon enough, however, for a small black thing burst through the opening in the door, causing Grandmother Pearl to jump back and shriek.

"Get out! Get out, you infernal creation!" she bellowed. Her face had gone scarlet, and Charlie would've sworn before a judge that the old woman actually snarled. As swiftly as it had appeared, however, the small creature dashed around the corner and was gone.

"What was that?" Charlie asked breathlessly.

Grandmother Pearl paused a moment before answering. Calmer now, she replied, "That is . . . our other cat. It is a nuisance. Once we thought we were rid of it, but it came back. It always comes back."

"I see," Charlie replied, though he didn't, really. At his feet, Talos relaxed.

"There now. Nothing to worry about," Grandmother Pearl said dully, and she pushed the door open the rest of the way.

Charlie stepped inside and found a simple bedroom that resembled his at home. There was a modest bed with a night table to one side and a short chest of drawers on the other, a small writing desk against the back wall, and a plain chair before the desk. On the bed rested Charlie's traveling bag, unopened. In the glow of a gas lamp, the room really did look perfectly safe. There wasn't even a window to give Charlie some terrifying view of whatever frozen wraiths might be haunting the winter night.

"Your things are on the bed, but you may use the chest for your clothes. There are extra blankets under the bed should you find it too cold to sleep," instructed Grandmother Pearl. "Is there anything else you might need?"

I need to go home was what Charlie thought, but what he said was, "I'm sure I have everything I need now, thank you. Only, will my sister be able to find me if she should get scared in the night?"

At this, Grandmother Pearl snorted. "Your sister will be fine," she said without a smile. "Should you find *yourself* scared in the night, you may knock upon the wall. My room is next door to yours."

"But—" Charlie began.

"I hear everything," said Grandmother Pearl as she turned to leave, "even at my age."

She left Charlie then, closing the door behind her. Before the door met its jamb, however, Charlie saw a flash of white fur and pale blue feline eyes. *He's keeping an eye on me,* he thought.

"Well, I'm keeping an eye on *you!*" Charlie muttered once the door was closed, though he ashamedly accepted that his four-legged foe had won for now.

I don't need to leave my room anyway, he tried to convince himself. *It's quite nice, really. Nothing to worry about at all.*

Of course, it would be then that the light would subtly flicker, that the wind would start up with its howling, and that sometimes those howls would sound like a ghostly child crying in the distance.

The hours passed like days as Charlie hid beneath the blankets. Not until his alarm clock went off in his hands did he believe he had survived the night, but even then, he was too afraid to emerge from his hiding place.

Soon, however, there was a tapping at his door. And the tapping was followed by the squeak of the handle turning. And the squeak was followed by the door's eerie groan. Charlie held his breath until he thought he would faint as the floor squealed under slow footsteps.

And then . . .

"WAKE UP! WAKE UP, CHARLIE-O! IT'S TIME TO START THE MORRRNIIING!"

"Georgie!" Charlie shouted as he threw off the blankets to find his sister standing there, giggling. "You nearly scared me to death! I thought you were someone else."

He was too embarrassed to admit he feared that that someone was Grandmother Pearl come to feed him to her cat.

"Sorry. That wasn't very polite of me. I thought maybe you'd slept late for once," Georgie said regretfully, "but you didn't sleep at all, did you?"

Charlie shook his head. "As usual," he said. "I'm sure you slept just fine. As usual."

"Actually, no. I slept, that is, but not very fine," Georgie quietly replied. She frowned and sat down on the edge of the bed. "I had the most awful nightmare about Mama."

"What did you dream?" Charlie asked.

Georgie looked lost for a moment and chewed on her thumbnail. "I can't remember exactly," she said after a while. "Only that something terrible happened, and I couldn't help. I never have nightmares I can't find my way out of, Charlie."

But then she smiled again. "Oh well," she said with a shrug. "I'd much rather think about breakfast now anyway. Hurry up and get ready! I'm so hungry I could eat a table!"

She might as well have, for the hot breakfast they were promised turned out to be burnt oatmeal, coal-black toast, and tea that resembled tar. Before this dismal spread sat the two grandmothers, still in their nightdresses and robes. Neither offered any morning pleasantries nor even so much as looked up from the table at first. Perhaps it was the low light, but Charlie thought they looked a little withered and oddly gray.

"We must be quite the sight this morning, mustn't we, your Grandmother Pearl and me?" said Grandmother Opal in a particularly frail voice. When she looked up at the children, Charlie saw there were deep, dark circles under her eyes.

Charlie struggled for something kind to say.

"It's only lack of sleep, dear. I'm afraid we both missed our naps yesterday," Grandmother Opal explained. "We would have slept in this morning, but we so very much wanted to be here when you awoke."

"This is our time to sleep," said Grandmother Pearl, who was staring down at a charred breadcrumb.

Charlie watched the two, thinking.

"We'll be all right on our own if you'd like to go back and get your rest, Grandmothers," said Georgie. She sat down and helped herself to the disastrous toast without even making a face. Charlie sat, too, but pretended to arrange a napkin rather than take food he knew he wouldn't eat.

Grandmother Opal smiled weakly. "If you'll pardon our manners, I promise we'll be in much better shape later in the day," she said.

"It's all right, Grandmothers. We understand. Might we be allowed to explore the house while you're sleeping?" asked Georgie.

Grandmother Pearl glanced sharply at Grandmother Opal, but the latter ignored the former. This exchange did not go unnoticed by Charlie, who was compiling evidence for a new theory about the elderly pair even as they spoke.

"Of course you may, but stay away from closed doors. They are closed for a reason," warned Grandmother Opal. Upon seeing Georgie's frown, she explained, "This house is old, my dear, and there are many dangerous places. You cannot be a proper explorer with a broken ankle."

"Yes, Grandmother Opal, I'll be careful," Georgie said. Charlie knew without looking that her fingers were crossed under the table, but the grandmothers were satisfied with her promise. With nods, they clumsily stood and hobbled away.

"I do hate to sleep through such a lovely morning," Charlie heard Grandmother Opal say to Grandmother Pearl even as lightning lit up the rural tundra.

"Soon it will all be different," said Grandmother Pearl.

"Vampires!" Charlie whispered once the women were out of earshot. "That explains it. They're vampires, and that's why they sleep in the morning!"

"What?! That's nonsense," Georgie scoffed, her mouth full of toast. "Nobody's a vampire, and I think the grandmothers are lovely."

"They're nice enough now, but I'm telling you there's something not right about them!" Charlie persisted. "So far, it all points to vampires. They can't cook, Georgie. What sort of grandmothers can't cook?"

"The ones who are better at things that aren't cooking?" Georgie suggested.

"Or the kind who haven't eaten human food in centuries!" Charlie returned. He grimaced as he watched Georgie devour the blackened breakfast. "How can you possibly eat that?"

Georgie shrugged and continued eating. "It tastes ghastly, it's true, but I'm a growing girl. Have to keep my strength up if I'm going exploring today."

Charlie felt hunger pangs, too, but the mess on the table dulled them a little.

"All right, so maybe they're not vampires," he said, "but you've got to agree they're not what you expected."

"They are a bit different," Georgie agreed, getting up from the table, "but it's not going to stop me from looking around. I think I shall start outside."

"Outside?! You didn't say anything about going outside earlier! You only said you were going to explore the house!" Charlie protested.

"I didn't say anything about staying *inside* the house, did I?" Georgie said with a wink.

Charlie was flabbergasted. "Did you not see that lightning? What if there's a thunder snowstorm? Or . . . or . . . an ice tornado?" he said. He wasn't sure if such things existed, but since the idea occurred to him so easily, he wasn't going to assume he'd made it up out of thin air.

"Well, if there is an *ice tornado*, I'll have quite a story to tell when I get back, won't I?" laughed Georgie. Seeing her brother's dismay, she added, "I'll stay close to the house, all right? If it gets ugly out there, I'll come back in straightaway."

Charlie struggled for words. He really didn't wish to be the overprotective brother again—but oh, the unknown! The terrible unknown!

"You could come with me," Georgie offered. "I don't mind. You'd just have to keep up is all."

"N-no, you should go," Charlie finally acquiesced. "I'll stay inside. Just keep close to the house like you said."

"All right," said Georgie. "If you get worried, open a window and yell for me. I'll come back inside before you can say Jack Robinson, I promise. No fingers crossed."

"No toes crossed, either?"

"No toes."

Charlie sighed and nodded, and then Georgie was off like a shot to her room, returning with her coat, hat, mittens, and her satchel full of all her detective tools.

"Tallyho, Charlie-O!" she said with a salute, and then she was out the door.

At that moment, Charlie became keenly aware of how alone he was. The grandmothers were asleep. His sister roamed somewhere out there in the frozen waste. And here he stood, too afraid to take so much as a step on his own.

"I'll just go and sit on the sofa until somebody comes back," he said to no one. So, Charlie sat, and he waited. He waited a bit longer, and then he waited longer still. But the more he waited, the more he noticed all the little sounds he'd been too distracted to hear before. Clocks ticking. The house settling. The cold wind moaning past the drafty windows.

This isn't making me feel one bit better, he thought.

That was when he discovered the staircase. Charlie wasn't sure how he hadn't seen it before, but there it was, as plain as day, cut into the hallway ahead. *There can't be anything pleasant up there*, he thought, but something nagged at him to go and have a peek all the same. When he stood at the base of the steps and looked up, however, he couldn't see anything but another flight of stairs. He thought, *If I just go up halfway, maybe I'll be able to see if there's any-*

thing dangerous up there, and then I'll come right back down, safe and sound.

At the halfway point, Charlie could just barely see the second floor, where he was happily surprised to catch a glimpse of what appeared to be a library. Nothing bad could ever be found in books, he told himself. Well, except for mold and stories that might give him nightmares. But if there was anything he could overlook his fears for, it was a nice, heavy encyclopedia. A tingling in his brain told him he just might find what he wished for if he'd only go up the rest of the stairs.

Once there, Charlie found the most beautiful house library he had ever seen. Granted, it was the only house library he'd ever seen, but it exceeded all his expectations of house libraries in every way. Here, a stained-glass window bathed the pristine white walls in soothing colors that almost gave the illusion of a sunny sky outdoors. Two plush leather armchairs begged for someone to curl up in them to read. True, it was a small library, but the ceilings were quite high, making room for tall cases that held thousands of books in all sizes.

And they were all encyclopedias and history books. Every one that Charlie saw.

Few worries could hold Charlie back now (that is to say, none of his usual worries were present), and he immediately flew to the thickest volume he could spot, hefting it with cautious glee from the shelf. It was a four-hundred-year-old guide to the creatures of the sea. Charlie had never seen anything like it. Its illustrations were all hand-drawn by master artists, every page a fragile masterpiece. He gently replaced the book and chose another. This one was all about the great kings and queens of bygone days. Though not as old as the sea book, there was something wonderfully ancient about it.

On and on Charlie went, book by book by book, too excited by all the magnificent histories and mysteries of the world to study any one volume for very long. He *was* starting to wonder if the shelves were stretching much longer than the room could contain, but this observation remained a mere itch in the back of his mind. The more Charlie browsed, the less he cared about his increasing distance from the entrance.

"*The Oh-nei-ro-criticon*," he read aloud from one worn spine. "*A Catalogue of Dreams*." Brimming with curiosity, he experienced only a moment's wariness before he pulled it from its place.

But behind the space once occupied by the tome, a furry white face stared back at him and then hissed. *Talos*. Charlie yelped and dropped the book.

"I'm sorry!" he said to the authors of the book as he turned and ran. And ran. And ran. It seemed he would *never* reach the door. He hadn't thought the library so enormous when he'd entered it, but he had other concerns now. Charlie ran so long that he thought his legs would give out, and they very nearly did. But with one last burst of strength, he made the final stretch to the doorway. He dove outside the library and flung himself onto the staircase, blind with terror as he fled. How he reached the bottom without falling, he didn't know, but he was extremely glad of it.

It's just a cat, he scolded himself as he ran back down the hall. *Who's afraid of a silly cat?* Finally, he reached the parlor and threw

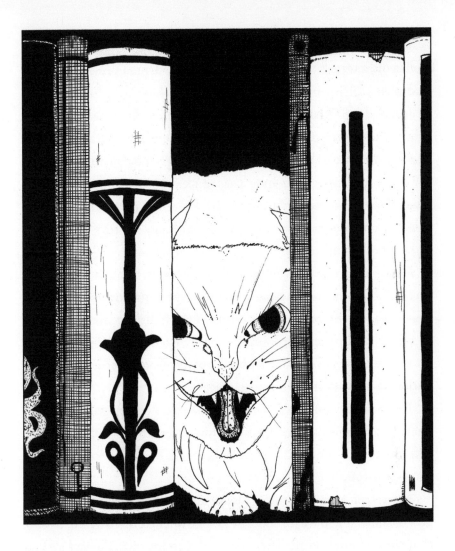

himself, panting and wheezing, onto the lumpy sofa with its thread-bare upholstery the color of rust.

Hold on a second, Charlie thought, jolting upright again. *This sofa was a dingy purplish color a few minutes ago.*

"What *now?*" he groaned.

The sofa wasn't the only thing different. Where previously there had been knitting in the rocking chair, now there lay a dull knife and whittled wood. Instead of an upright piano, a pump organ cast its shadow across the floor. The windows hid behind red drapes instead of plum ones, and the front door was most definitely smaller. To the unobservant, this might have passed as the very same parlor, but Charlie was nothing if not observant. He stood in a completely different room now; he was sure of it. What he wasn't sure of was how he came to be here and how he was going to get out.

Maybe I haven't gone far enough, he thought, though he couldn't imagine how this second parlor had escaped his notice before. Yet here it was on the ground floor ahead of the hall staircase. He simply couldn't have made a wrong turn. So, Charlie decided to continue on to the opposite hallway in hopes of eventually returning to the parlor he knew better.

This hallway contained the same faded wall coverings, similar daguerreotypes with those awful watching eyes, and lots of doors. But when he reached the end, he saw only a wall. No corners to turn. No exits to be found.

"Don't get scared, don't get scared, don't get scared," he whispered, squeezing his eyes shut. When he opened them again, he saw that the last door on the left, one similar to his own, glowed ever so faintly from underneath.

"Is—is someone there?" he asked, afraid of who or what might reply. "Grandmother Pearl? Grandmother Opal? Georgie?"

When no one answered, Charlie turned to leave, and he very well might have left without any incident whatsoever had this happened at any other time and to any other person. But in that moment, something furry brushed up against the backs of Charlie's legs, startling him so wildly that he flailed like laundry in a windstorm until he lost his balance and stumbled backward into the door. And this door had not been properly latched.

As the door flung open and took him with it, Charlie caught a glimpse out the corner of his eye of the mysterious black cat dashing away in a blur. Then *crash!* Charlie was on his back. *I've done it now,* he thought. *I've gone and broken my ribs. Probably punctured a lung. It's all over for me.*

But he hadn't broken his ribs or punctured any lungs, and nothing was all over for him quite yet. In fact, Charlie had landed in a pile of small sweaters and coats. *Whose room was this?* he thought as he looked around, for all about him lay heaps of clothing and toys. Rather old ones, too, judging by the state of the things. There was a rusty tin train set, a dented-up pair of ice skates, a wooden dog with a head that wobbled on an overstretched spring, to name a few.

Rummaging carefully through the relics, Charlie forgot all about the black cat and the faint light he'd seen before, now nowhere to be found. There were so many toys here that when he stood up, some of the piles went all the way up to his waist. There must have been hundreds! But where had they all come from? To whom had they belonged?

An idea formed in Charlie's mind then. An idea that was confirmed for him when he pulled a tarnished silver pocket watch from a torn-up boot. On the back of the watch was an engraving that read *For Chris.*

Father's name had been Christopher.

Charlie felt an ache somewhere in the neighborhood of his heart, followed by something prickly in his eyes. The feeling was one most people would identify as the start of tears but that Charlie hadn't allowed himself to experience in many years. *What's the matter with my eyes?* he thought as they began to leak. But just when he was reacquainting himself with this particular sensation, something hooked onto the back of his shirt collar. In an instant, Charlie was yanked backward, heels scraping the floor, before he could even think to scream.

CHAPTER FOUR

THE OLD TREE

Charlie found himself flat on his back, only to be jerked to his feet again by a person of remarkable strength. He expected to encounter some hulking monster the likes of Frankenstein's creation, but there, gripping his shoulder with one hooked hand and seething with a white-hot fury, stood no one but Grandmother Pearl.

"Who told you that you were allowed to go in there? *Who told you?*" she roared, absolutely shaking with rage.

It took Charlie a few breaths before he could find the words to answer.

"I didn't mean to!" he eventually said. "I fell and—and—and the door was open! Honest!"

"You should have fallen back out, then," the old woman snarled in reply. She unhooked herself from Charlie's shoulder and resumed her usual stooped posture. *How could someone so frail be so strong?* Charlie thought, but then he felt ashamed.

"I'm sorry," he said quietly, and then, "I understand."

"Eh?" squawked Grandmother Pearl, cupping one ear.

"I s-said I understand," Charlie repeated. "You must be my father's mother, and those things in there . . . they were Father's, too, weren't they? Mother never told us before we came, you see. I didn't know."

A visible calm came over Grandmother Pearl just then, and it seemed as though her wrath had passed. But the moment ended when she wrapped her ancient fingers around Charlie's arm and marched him back to his bedroom, muttering to herself the whole way. "Won't like this one bit. No, no, she won't. Going to be my death, this one!"

Charlie felt absolutely rotten. He did wonder, in the back of his mind, how he could have missed certain twists and turns in the hallway before, but he was too burdened by heavier thoughts to care very much now.

"You'll stay in there until you've thought about what you've done!" ordered Grandmother Pearl when they came to his room, adding before she left him, "No lunch for bad kiddies! No, not a bite!"

But I'm not a bad kiddie, thought Charlie. He sat down on the squeaky bed and sank his chin into his hands. *I didn't even want to go into that smelly old room. I wouldn't have gotten so lost if this house made any sense at all. The room was probably full of tetanus anyway. I'm lucky nothing scratched me. I really am.*

For all Charlie's bitterness, however, he couldn't help feeling sorry for Grandmother Pearl. To lose someone you love is a dreadful thing.

When it happened to Charlie, he felt like his heart had cracked into a thousand pieces. Since then, he'd imagined heavy chains wrapped around that fractured heart of his to hold all the pieces in place. He had imagined it so often that he really felt the weight of them sometimes, and now he couldn't figure out how to remove them when he wanted to. Charlie wondered if Grandmother Pearl wore the same chains.

The door opened again later, but it was Grandmother Opal this time. The color had returned to her cheeks since her morning nap, and she seemed more like the pleasant lady Charlie had met the night before, if a bit solemn. She sat down beside him and tried to make lighthearted conversation.

"What a funny little thing," she mused, taking Charlie's alarm clock and tapping one of its bells. "Do you remember who gave it to you?"

Charlie didn't want to answer. And anyway, it was clear to him that Grandmother Opal wasn't there to talk about clocks.

"I didn't mean to go into that room," he mumbled.

Grandmother Opal sighed and replaced the clock. "Charlie, you mustn't blame yourself," she said with a sad smile. "Grandmother Pearl wasn't right to scold you. If she wanted the room left alone, she ought to have made sure she locked it. I told her as much, but it's hard for her, you know."

Charlie nodded but couldn't bring himself to look up from his knees. He'd never been scolded so harshly by anyone before, and the memory of it still stung despite the comforting words of the kinder grandmother.

"Come now, no need to be so down in the mouth! I'll bring you your lunch soon," Grandmother Opal said with a wink. "Better to stay in here for now, though, until Grandmother Pearl's mood has bettered. Isn't there anything else I can do to cheer you up?"

Charlie brightened a bit then. "Might I have a sheet of paper and something to write with?" he asked. "I would like to write a letter to Mother. She'll probably be bored in the hospital without any company."

If she's awake, he thought.

Grandmother Opal sighed again. "I'm afraid we never know when the postman will come our way next. We see so little of him these days," she said, idly twisting her great black ring around her finger, "but don't you worry a fig. Soon you'll be having so much fun you'll forget all about your mother!"

Just as Grandmother Opal rose to go, a snow-drenched Georgie came bounding in, still in her coat and mittens. She'd have barreled right into the old woman without even noticing had Grandmother Opal not stepped out of the way just in time.

"There you are, Charlie-O!" Georgie exclaimed. "I've been looking all over for you!"

"Since when? I've been right here for the past hour," said Charlie.

"Well, you can't blame me for forgetting where your room is. But that's not what I'm trying to tell you!" said Georgie, as out of patience as she was of breath. "I'm trying to tell you what I found outside!"

"Pray, what were you doing out of doors?" interrupted Grandmother Opal.

"I'm afraid that's my fault, too," Charlie regretfully volunteered.

"I told her she could go, but I did make her promise to stay close to the house."

"And did you?" Grandmother Opal asked Georgie.

"Well . . . ," said Georgie as she pretended to examine the hem of her coat, "he didn't say *how* close."

"Georgie!" Charlie snapped. Grandmother Opal only chuckled.

Georgie ignored them both. "Look what I found hidden in a hole in that old tree!" she said, and she lifted a foot to show off one of a pair of weathered, slightly oversized black rain boots. "Can I keep them, Grandmother Opal? They're ever so much nicer than mine. Whose were they?"

Grandmother Opal blinked, and her smile began losing its luster. "They were mine when I was not much older than you," she said stiffly, "but you shouldn't go to the tree again, dearest. It isn't a good place for children."

"Why not?" Georgie asked. "Is it because of the animal tracks?"

"There were *animal tracks?*" Charlie squeaked.

"Big ones! With gigantic claws!" Georgie answered, playfully scratching at the air and growling.

"Wolves," Grandmother Opal said very seriously. "Oh, don't be frightened! They never come close to the house, but something about that tree draws them to it. Keep away from it, dear heart. I wouldn't want any nasty creatures gobbling up such a clever little girl before her time!"

On this ominous note, Grandmother Opal left the children alone.

"You promised," Charlie said, hurt.

"I know," said Georgie with true remorse, "but you have to believe me, Charlie, I didn't mean to stray so far! I don't even know how I got there! One minute I was investigating a little door on the side of the house. The next minute—*whoosh!*—I turned around and there was fog everywhere. I couldn't find my own hand in front of my face! I walked all around for ages and ages and *ages* before the fog went away, and when it did, I was miles from the house!"

"Miles?!"

"Acres maybe. How long is a mile again?" Georgie tried to think. Then, "But never mind that. Tell me you believe me! I tried really, really hard to keep my promise. It was almost like the house *wanted* me to get lost."

A new wrinkle creased Charlie's brow then. "The thing is, I do believe you," he said. "Something very similar just happened to me, as a matter of fact."

"Really?" asked Georgie.

Charlie leaned in close. "Upstairs, there's a library, and I—" he began in a whisper, but he was interrupted by the return of Grandmother Opal.

"Lu-unch!" she sang, and she placed before Charlie a tray with two grilled cheese sandwiches, each halved into neat triangles. The cheese was on the outside of the bread rather than the inside, and there was a widening pool of distressingly black grease creeping to the edges of the plate, but his stomach rumbled greedily nonetheless. It had been some time since he'd eaten.

"Grandmother Opal," Georgie began as Charlie devoured his lunch, "what's the little door on the side of the house?"

"I beg your pardon?" asked Grandmother Opal.

"The *little* door," Georgie repeated with great exasperation. "It's on the east side of the house, and it's locked. Where does it lead?"

"Only to the fruit cellar," Grandmother Opal tersely replied. "There's nothing down there but rats and spoiled food. You've no need to go poking around there again."

"Oh," said Georgie, disappointed.

Grandmother Opal's smile returned, and she took Georgie's hand. "Come along, young lady," she said as she led her from the room. "I've prepared your lunch in the kitchen. Let us leave your brother to enjoy his sandwiches in peace."

"When will I be allowed to leave?" Charlie tried to ask, but his mouth was full of oily cheese and wrong-side-out bread, so all he could manage was a slur of syllables that no one heard as his door groaned to a close.

The answer to Charlie's question was this: not for many hours. And in those hours, he paced to and fro, jumping a little at every squealing complaint of the floorboards. He pressed his ear to each wall to listen for anything suspicious, but that never does any good when *every* sound is suspicious. When he finally summoned a little courage, he tried the door handle and found to his dismay that it was locked. To tell it truly, he also felt somewhat relieved. If he wasn't able to leave the room, he reasoned, no one would think him a coward for staying put. The troubling question that remained was *why* anyone would need to lock a twelve-year-old boy in his room. Charlie wasn't one of those hooligans who smash windows or carve curse words into their school desks. He'd simply tripped over a cat and stumbled into a room where he wasn't wanted.

"I told you I was sorry, Grandmother Pearl," he grumbled.

It wasn't until nearly eight in the evening that Charlie heard the jangle of keys. With Talos at her side as usual, Grandmother Pearl had come to fetch him for dinner. She apologized for her earlier severity, but it didn't sound very sincere to Charlie. Rather, it was as if someone had put her up to it, and when the grandmother's gaze kept darting down at the cat as she spoke, Charlie half wondered if that someone was Talos.

He's keeping an eye on her *now and not me,* Charlie thought, but then he shook his head and thought, *That's ridiculous. He's a cat. A gosh-darn cat. Unless . . .*

There was a new idea swirling around the kettle of Charlie's brain. It was ludicrous to be sure. Indeed, it was so out of the realm of possibility that he wouldn't put the idea into words at first. But when Georgie didn't show up for dinner—stomach complaints, Grandmother Opal said—Charlie began to wonder more seriously.

Witches, he thought. *Could they be? They've already got an enchanted cat. They could have made Georgie ill. They could have put the spell on Mother that made her send us here. By gosh! That would explain everything!*

"May I be excused, Grandmothers?" Charlie asked after pushing around the board-stiff roast a little. "I'd like to check on my sister and see if she's all right."

"But you've barely touched your dinner!" Grandmother Opal complained.

"It is necessary for children to eat," agreed Grandmother Pearl.

Charlie felt nervous sweat beading up on his forehead. "I'm really not hungry," he fibbed. "Actually, I think I have the same stomach bug."

It was an excuse that turned out to be a mistake.

"If you're ill as well, then you'd best get back to bed and rest," said Grandmother Opal. Before Charlie could protest, Grandmother Pearl stood up and clamped her hand onto his shoulder.

"Come along to bed," she said in a flat voice.

"Look, if you could just tell me where Georgie's room is, I'm sure I can find my own way," Charlie said to no avail.

"You haven't been sleeping," said Grandmother Pearl. "That's what's the matter with you. If you don't sleep, you won't be of use to anybody, will you?"

"Don't worry, dear. I'll look after your sister," Grandmother Opal promised.

Charlie reluctantly followed Grandmother Pearl to his room again, shouting at himself inside his head the whole time. *Break away! Find Georgie! Find Georgie and flee before the witches eat you both and use your bones for potions!*

But by the time they reached his room, his frantic fears had quieted to dull concerns. The grandmothers couldn't be witches. Witches weren't real, and the grandmothers were family. Grandmother Pearl had been Father's mother, and Father's mother would naturally be protective of his belongings. It was the only thing that made sense. Even if the grandmothers *were* witches, what good was an easily frightened boy like himself against them? But they weren't witches. They couldn't be. Witches weren't real, and the grandmothers were family.

That night, the wind cried like ghost children again, and sometimes it scratched along the outer walls with whatever debris it had
picked up from the snow. Bits of bark from the old tree, perhaps,
or small bones from the wolves' last dinner. *Grandmother Opal said
the wolves never come to the house,* Charlie told himself even as he
huddled beneath the blankets.

Among the sounds of wailing and scratching came lower tones
that did not die with the icy gusts. It sounded like two people bickering. Men or women, he couldn't discern, but there was nothing

pleasant about it. *It's only my imagination*, Charlie thought with his eyes squeezed shut. Then there was another sound. A strange sound that went like this: *Thunk! Shiffffffft . . . Thunk! Shiffffffft . . .* Like a shovel being driven into the hard earth and discarding its purchase over and over again.

It was not the wind. No, it most certainly was not, and Charlie knew he couldn't go on pretending that it was. *Someone's digging a hole*, he thought, *but what could they possibly be planting at this hour? Or burying?*

Charlie threw off the blankets and sat up, eyes wide with panic. *Oh no*, he thought.

"Georgie!" he called, and he jumped from the bed and dashed to the door only to find it locked again. With a cry of frustration, he turned and pounded on the wall he shared with Grandmother Pearl. He pounded it so hard that his fists turned purple.

"Let me out!" he shouted, his heart fluttering faster than a hummingbird's wings. "You let me out right now, you witch! What have you done with my sister?"

But no one answered.

No one came.

Charlie must have fainted. He opened his eyes, not aware he'd even closed them, only to be blinded by the blaze of a rising sun. Shielding his face from the glare, he waited for clarity to set in. The shouting in the night, the digging. Could it have been a dream? Charlie saw that he lay in bed, but he didn't feel like he'd slept. His eyes ached with the rawness of insomnia, his fists still hot from his desperate pounding upon the wall. Terrible dreams were nothing new to him, but this . . .

Another thought occurred to Charlie then, and he slowly lowered his arm, letting the sun's rays burn into his eyes. *Since when,* he wondered, *did this room have a window?*

Charlie did the only thing that made sense to him at confounding times like these and reached for his alarm clock. To his horror, his hand grasped nothing but air.

"What?" he muttered, staring stupidly at the bare tabletop as if looking harder would reveal what was surely there. But there was no denying it. It was gone. His beloved alarm clock, the one thing he had always believed he could count on, was nowhere in sight.

Charlie ransacked his room as much as one can ransack such meager quarters, yet the clock was not to be found. "Where is it? What've they done with it?" he grumbled. Just before he gave up hope, he scrambled to the dresser and, though it was an unlikely place for anyone to put a bedside clock, he pulled out all the drawers.

He didn't find what he sought, but what he did find confused him greatly. All of his clothes were missing, and in their place were drab gray uniforms: button-down shirts and something like pajama pants. There were several pairs of them, and all were the same cheerless gray.

"What's going on around here?" Charlie asked out loud.

"Your clothes needed washing," said a frail voice behind him, "and gray is a fitting color for a young man."

Exactly *when* Grandmother Pearl had come in, Charlie had no idea, but her sickly pallor startled him as much as her sudden arrival. She looked as gray as the clothes in the dresser, and she was more horribly gaunt than the morning before. The dark puffiness under her eyes made her look like an elderly lizard. But Charlie had seen her strength, and he wasn't falling for the weak old grandmother act now. Even if she was his grandmother—and he wasn't entirely convinced—that didn't mean she wasn't up to something sinister.

"All right, where is my sister?" he asked, doing his best to keep his voice steady.

"Down at breakfast, I suppose," Grandmother Pearl said before she issued a bone-rattling cough into a crumpled handkerchief. "What do you remember about her?"

Another strange question. Charlie chose not to answer.

"And my alarm clock?" he said.

"Your what, boy?"

"My alarm clock. It was here, and now it's not. It's important to me. Did you take it when you took my clothes?"

Grandmother Pearl shook her head and irritably waved Charlie away. "It's time for my morning nap. I'm too old and too tired to find your toys before my nap," she said, and she drifted away without even closing the door.

There were many things Charlie wanted to shout after her, but fear and decorum prevented him. Instead, he threw on his slippers and ran down to the kitchen to see if Grandmother Pearl spoke the truth. To his great relief, Georgie was indeed there and fortunately alone. Strangely, she was also scooping burnt biscuits from a platter and cramming them into the pockets of her own gray uniform.

"Thank heavens, you're alive!" Charlie exclaimed. "But what in the blue blazes are you doing?"

Georgie motioned for him to be silent. "They took my detective bag, so I have to use these pockets. I'm packing some for you, too. Now, hush!" she said. "The grandmothers are napping, and I don't want them to wake up and catch us."

"Catch us?"

But Georgie only put her finger to her lips and returned to her task of pilfering food.

"Are we going somewhere?" Charlie whispered. "Because if that's your big idea, well, you know what I'm going to say."

"For once in our lives, just trust me!" Georgie returned. Then she folded her arms across her chest and threatened, "I'm going out there anyway, you know, so you might as well come along to keep me out of trouble!"

A dozen reasons for why this was a bad idea sat in Charlie's throat just waiting to be spoken, but he already knew he'd lost this fight. Georgie was obviously up to no good, and Charlie couldn't protect her from inside the house. Now he had no choice but to accompany her, which he knew was exactly what she had planned.

"Why do you always have to be so clever?" Charlie grumbled.

Georgie grinned. "They took our coats, too," she said, "but I know where we can find some."

*   *   *

The outside sky did not match the view from Charlie's window, a window he decided he simply must have failed to notice before. What sun there was cowered behind a wall of clouds so dark it looked as though dusk had already begun with nightfall fast on its heels. *The darkness comes earlier and earlier every day,* Charlie thought, *and it's even colder than ever.*

In the chill, the children's breath curled out of them like smoke, and Charlie was grateful for the fur coats they'd found in a hall closet, even if these were women's coats and reeked of mothballs, too. He was not so grateful to be outside. Often had he thought of running away to the nearest town, but now was not that time. Not without provisions or any kind of plan. Not while he was in his pajamas and slippers.

"All right, you've gotten me as far as the porch. Tell me what this is all about before I lose my nerve and take us both back inside," Charlie said through his teeth. It was a hollow threat, of course, but he hoped Georgie would at least humor him.

"I found a door on the side of the house yesterday," his sister said, munching on a biscuit. "Grandmother Opal says it's nothing, but I don't believe her."

"You mean the cellar door?"

"How did you know?"

"You told me about it yesterday," said Charlie. "You were looking at it when you got lost in the fog, and you wound up at the old tree."

"You're misremembering," said Georgie. "I haven't even been out to the old tree yet. I'd never hear the end of it from you if I did!"

71

Charlie was flummoxed. "But that's where you found the boots you're wearing right now," he insisted. "Don't you remember?"

Georgie looked down at her oversized boots all caked with dirty snow, and she frowned. "Mama gave me these," she said uncertainly. "She did. I *know* she did. Didn't she, Charlie?"

She looked to her brother for confirmation. When it didn't come, she scowled. "Oh, stop making up stories and follow me!" she snapped. "What does it matter if I told you about the door before or not? I want you to *see* it!"

Charlie begrudgingly followed his sister around the house, looking over his shoulder every time there was even the slightest sound that didn't come from their own trudging feet. Around and around the children plodded, twice around the house and halfway back the other way. Poor Charlie's slippers were soaked with icy slush, and to make matters worse, there were no signs of any mysterious little door, cellar or otherwise.

"It must be here somewhere!" said Georgie, plunging one foot deep into the snow in a stomp of frustration.

"You said it was on the east side of the house, remember?" Charlie gently reminded her.

"But we've *been* to the east side. Twice!" Georgie whined. "How can a door just disappear?"

Charlie felt the hair standing up on the back of his neck at the thought, and a shudder shook him through and through. "The hallways seem to do that, too," he said, pulling his coat tighter. He looked up at the house and studied its features. This was the first time he'd really looked at it. It didn't seem quite so large on the outside as it did on the inside, and its once-white exterior was in desperate need of repainting. The twin windows at its peak and the windows beside the door below made it look like it had a watchful face with a giant maw full of teeth. Charlie wondered if houses could ever be living beings.

"What do you think it would say if it could talk?" Charlie asked.

But Georgie didn't answer. Georgie was gone.

"Georgie?" Charlie squeaked. There wasn't any reply. *It's happening,* he thought. *Everything I've feared the most. I looked away for one second, and now I've lost everyone!*

"Georgie Louise!" Charlie shouted now, running. "If this is a game, I'm going to tell Mother when we're home again, and she'll be terribly disappointed in you!"

But Charlie was far more frightened than angry; the tremor in his voice would've given that away to a pure stranger. He thought back to what Georgie had said before, and he felt like his stomach was twisting up in knots. "It was almost like the house wanted me to get lost," she had said. He had felt that way, too, but he'd been careless all the same.

"Georgie!"

Charlie ran all around the house, screaming his sister's name until he was hoarse and then screaming it again anyway. He ran a dozen circles around the house in search of her, but with the snow falling heavier every second, there was little evidence that she had been there at all. *What if that wasn't a dream last night?* he thought as he ran around again. *What if it really was digging I heard, and she fell into a hole, and now the snow is falling so fast she's already—*

"Charlie!" cried a voice he knew, and he turned to find Georgie running toward him from just around the corner.

"Georgie! Where were you?" he yelled. "I was looking everywhere for you! Why didn't you answer when I called? I thought you'd been buried alive or—"

He stopped when he saw that Georgie, very much out of character, was crying.

"I didn't hear you!" she sobbed. "I looked all over, and you weren't there! I called and called and called for you, but you never answered!"

Both of them stopped and stared at one another. Neither said a word, but Charlie knew that Georgie was thinking the same thing as he. *It's the house,* he thought. *The house is trying to separate us.*

It was then that Charlie felt the distinct sensation of being watched. His immediate suspicion was the dreaded white cat, but when he looked out the corner of his eye, he glimpsed not Talos, but something small and black in the distance. He gestured for Georgie to be quiet as he turned and peered into the gathering fog.

Some yards away, the blurry shape of the black cat waited, partially concealed by a bright twinkle of light near its chest. But as soon as Charlie understood what he saw, the unnamed cat turned tail and ran away. It was always popping up in the oddest places and always at the oddest times, Charlie thought. Just out of sight. Behind his legs. Zipping out of doors before he could really see it and getting him into trouble. Grandmother Pearl and Talos both hated the animal, but that made Charlie all the more determined to find it.

"Charlie? What's wrong?" Georgie asked.

"I've got to follow that cat," Charlie said, grabbing his sister's hand. "Come with me, and don't let go!"

"What cat? I don't see any cats. Charlie, where are we going?" Georgie shouted as they ran farther and farther from the house to chase after a blurry black dot.

"There's definitely a cat, and it's been sneaking up on me. Something tells me it wants to be followed," Charlie explained.

"You're making me nervous, Charlie!"

"Come on. It'll be exciting!"

Never in all his days would Charlie have thought he'd have to convince his sister to do something daring. For once, he was the brave one. What a strange notion it was! And a worrying one, too.

Then, just like that, the black cat vanished.

"Not again!" Charlie groaned. He stopped and looked all around, but if the cat was anywhere nearby, it was completely obscured by the fog. Just up ahead, however, something huge loomed from the swirls of mist. It was tall, he could tell, with twisting arms that reached out in one direction like a claw.

The old tree.

It was at that moment that he realized they had run all that way into fog as thick as soup with the threat of untold horrors all around them, and yet he hadn't been afraid even once. It was unfortunately a fleeting realization. *Wolves!* he remembered with sudden dizziness. *How could I have forgotten the wolves? We'll be eaten for sure! Oh, what have I done?*

"I *have* been here. I remember now," Georgie whispered beside him. "I really think we should go back. We can find the way if we try. Let's go, Charlie. Please!"

Charlie gulped, his throat as dry as last night's roast. "Yes!" was all he managed to say.

But another figure soon emerged from the mist, all fragile-looking and ill. In her arms was curled a white cat with startling blue eyes. Neither cat nor woman looked pleased to see them.

CHAPTER FIVE

BEHIND THE LITTLE DOOR

If Grandmother Pearl felt the bitter cold, she certainly didn't show it as she shoved the children toward the house. "You were told not to go to the tree. You were told!" she spat. Behind them Talos stalked, invisible in the snow but for his searing eyes.

"Disobedient little somethings you are!" the grandmother continued. "You'll scrub the parlor floors for this!"

And scrub they did. All day they scrubbed. Charlie and Georgie scrubbed the floors, the walls, the woodwork, and every other surface until their hands were raw and their knees ached. If they stopped for so much as a second, Talos mewed at Grandmother Pearl, who immediately screeched at them to pick up the pace. Charlie had never much cared for the white cat, but now he was sure he hated it.

Of course, Grandmother Opal was nowhere in sight. Charlie figured she must have been napping again. It was something the grandmothers did a lot, he noted with suspicion. Georgie would blame it on their advanced years, but Charlie wasn't convinced. *It's either because they're witches who aren't used to the sunlight,* he thought, *or because they're awful old ladies who aren't used to children.* But perhaps that wasn't fair, he considered. Grandmother Opal, at least, had always been kind to them. *Maybe the truth is that Grandmother Pearl keeps her locked up in her room during the day,* he theorized, *just to be mean.*

It must have been half past two in the afternoon when Grandmother Opal finally surfaced, and Grandmother Pearl left to attend to some other business of the house.

"Oh, Grandmother Opal!" Georgie cried. She jumped up and hugged her, inadvertently splashing the poor woman with soapy water from her scrubbing brush.

"There, there, my poor dears," Grandmother Opal soothed. "What has mean old Grandmother Pearl done to you now?"

The children explained, and the grandmother nodded, sometimes tsking and shaking her head.

"My, my," she said when they concluded their hysterical tale. "I *am* sorry about Grandmother Pearl's harshness. She really doesn't mean to be so cruel. She's only trying, in her own way, to look out for you! It's a pity she forgets she was once a child herself. But . . ."

She moved to a closet that, of course, Charlie had never observed before. *That happens a lot around here.*

"I have something that will lighten your burden!" Grandmother Opal announced. And from the mysterious closet she wheeled out a cart, atop which sat a tall, bulky shape with a white sheet draped over it.

"Ta-da!" she sang as she whipped the sheet off the shape, which turned out to be a phonograph with a spectacularly large brass horn.

"Oh!" Charlie exclaimed. He had seen phonographs in advertisements, but he'd never actually been in front of one before. Once, he had thought them something only the very rich could afford, but here one was. It looked peculiarly old, he thought, but there were times he thought himself growing older every time he looked in the washroom mirror. It seemed to be a side effect of living in this house.

"Is it real?" Georgie excitedly asked. "Can we play it?"

"Of course you can!" Grandmother Opal laughed, and from a shelf in the cart, she produced a black disk as large as a dinner plate. This she placed upon the phonograph's spindle. After she moved some parts and turned its crank a few times, the machine began to whir, the disk began to spin, and out from the horn came a tinkling piano tune unlike anything the children had heard before. Why, it was magnificent! Even Charlie had to marvel at the wonder of it. Georgie laughed and jumped and twirled around with the tune. Charlie smiled in spite of himself and couldn't help but tap his foot in time.

"I'm afraid I can't lift your punishment without getting Grandmother Pearl's dander up, but I hope this will make your work a *teensy* bit more fun," Grandmother Opal said with a wink. "Now, how about some lunch? You poor creatures must be half starved!"

With that, she went off to the kitchen to prepare a meal that would probably be terrible. For the moment, though, it didn't matter as much.

"If only Mother could see this," Charlie wished. "It's almost like she's playing for us inside that box!"

"I'd almost forgotten Mama played the piano," Georgie said, pirouetting.

Charlie's pulse nearly died at the sound of this. "You forgot Mother played the piano?!" he said.

"Well, it's not as if she plays very often," said Georgie with a jump and a skip.

"Not as if she— Georgie!" said Charlie, stunned. "She's a piano *teacher*!"

Georgie hummed to herself along with the music and continued to dance, unperturbed by Charlie's horror.

"Sometimes I can't remember what she looks like," she admitted, but then she promptly stopped dancing and frowned.

"I've forgotten Mama," she said with a lost expression. "That's bad, isn't it, Charlie?"

It was worse than bad. The children had barely been away from home three days—far too soon to be so forgetful, and this was hardly the first instance. *Was it something in the food?* Charlie wondered. *It couldn't have been,* he told himself, for he had eaten it, too, yet he had forgotten nothing as far as he knew. The air? The water? No and no again. Brother and sister had shared everything, but only Georgie was slipping farther and farther away. *This is Grandmother Pearl's doing,* he thought. *Somehow it* has *to be.*

"Let's turn off the music. I don't like it anymore," he said.

"Yes. Yes, let's," Georgie anxiously agreed.

As soon as Charlie stopped the phonograph, he heard muffled voices coming from elsewhere in the house.

"Do you hear that?" he whispered. Georgie nodded.

The voices were deep and gruff and angry, like those that Charlie had heard the night of the shoveling. He had finally convinced himself those sounds were his imagination, but now his worries were refreshed. Before he had time to voice his fears, however, Georgie was sprinting down the hall ahead of them—directly to the source of the voices.

"Georgie! Come back!" Charlie hissed, but of course she wouldn't. Charlie silently screamed and pulled at his hair in frustration before he took off after his stubborn sister. When he caught up to her, he found her pulling off her boots, ready to sneak up a stairwell. She held a finger to her lips and then wordlessly urged him to doff his own shoes. This he did because, as usual, she hadn't left him much choice. The two of them then tiptoed in their stocking feet toward the voices, which led them to a closed door.

"*Listen!*" Georgie mouthed, pressing her ear to it. Charlie, too, listened, and what he heard electrified the very hair on the back of his neck.

"*. . . your fault if this is our undoing!*" snapped one of the voices.

"*Can't stay awake so long, General. Not fair, it is. Not fair!*" said the other.

Charlie and Georgie gaped at one another.

"*What if they'd damaged the harvest tree?*" the bickering continued.

"*Well, they didn't. And they wouldn't if we'd just take them down now and get it over with!*"

"*It's too soon, and you know that! We have to ease them into it. If we rush things, we'll scare them, and then they'll end up rotten! It's the entire reason we're here, you dunderhead. Do you want to have to start all over again?*"

"*But, General—*"

"She has already warned us twice, fool! I swear by the figment, if you say another word, I shall feed you to the phantoms myself!"

Charlie felt a chill and looked down the hall to catch a silhouette of a particularly fluffy cat. *Talos.* Straightaway, Charlie grabbed his sister by the arm and fled with her back down to the parlor, stopping only once to snatch their shoes from the base of the stairs. He thanked the heavens Georgie didn't make a noisy fuss about the retreat. Equally thankful was he that they'd managed to flee without getting lost or being followed.

"Why did we run?" Georgie asked when they returned.

"It just seemed like the right time," Charlie answered. He didn't want to tell her that he feared the house cat was a spy.

Back in the parlor, the children returned to their chores in the hope that no one would know they'd ever left. After what they had heard, however, every task was difficult to maintain without distraction.

"Who do you think they were?" Georgie asked in a hushed voice as she polished an urn, rubbing the same spot so many times it was a wonder she didn't wear it right through. "Do you think the grandmothers are in some kind of trouble?"

"I don't know, but I'm certain those people were talking about us. They *had* to have been," Charlie said while he dusted the piano.

"How do you know that? I don't even know what a harvest tree is!" said Georgie.

Charlie glanced nervously in the direction of the kitchen, where Grandmother Opal had been preparing lunch.

"It's got to be the old tree out there," he whispered. "The one where Grandmother Pearl found us. They talked about a 'she.' Georgie, there's only one person that could be!"

"Who, Charlie? Who?"

"Grandmother Pearl!"

Georgie processed the idea for a few seconds and then shook her head. "Don't be silly," she said. "Grandmother Pearl's not very nice, but she's not a villain. And anyway, we haven't been out to that old tree yet. At least I haven't. Did you turn brave while I wasn't looking, Charlie-O?"

She's forgotten again, thought Charlie. *It's happening faster and faster with every passing hour.*

Before he could say anything, however, he heard footsteps approaching from the very same hall they'd just escaped. Quick as a whip, he whirled around to return to his task of dusting. Soon after, Grandmother Pearl and Talos entered the room. Then, to Charlie's surprise, Grandmother Opal as well.

"Grandmother Opal, I thought you were in the kitchen," Charlie blurted before his reason could stop him. *Stupid,* he thought. *You've panicked again, and now they'll know you're paying attention!*

"Oh goodness!" Grandmother Opal laughed. "You poor dears were so busy slaving away for Grandmother Pearl that you didn't see me come through. Isn't that funny, Grandmother Pearl?"

"Ha," said Grandmother Pearl before she grunted and sat down in the rocking chair, scowling.

"Lunch will be along shortly," said Grandmother Opal, fidgeting with her ring. "We, er, had unfortunate business with some hired men to deal with. I've always said that if you want something done properly, you've got to do it yourself. Isn't that right, sister?"

Grandmother Pearl's only answer was the *creak, creak, creak* of the rocking chair.

Charlie didn't know what to make of this turn of events. The conversation they'd heard did not sound like business talk with employees, but he couldn't make heads or tails of what they'd said either way. Why, he wondered, had he never seen these hired hands? What secret was Grandmother Opal hiding for her sister?

Charlie looked worriedly at Georgie. She seemed to be lost in her own world now, still polishing that same spot on the urn. What was happening to her? Why couldn't she hold anything in her head anymore? Charlie's own head ached. His head always ached these days. He was so frightened he could scarcely breathe.

The rest of the children's day was filled with chores, terrible food, and more chores after that. And as the hour grew late, new troubles plagued Charlie's already weary mind. Soon, he knew, they would be taken off to their rooms to sleep, but after everything they had experienced today, he couldn't possibly let Georgie out of his sight again. But what could he do? How could he protect his sister in this house? If they ran away, they'd die of the cold or worse—they'd be eaten by wolves.

"Time for bed!" Grandmother Pearl barked, precisely as Charlie had predicted.

"I'm really not tired," Charlie said. He was, in truth, exhausted—so exhausted that his bones felt like anvils, and his eyes watered and stung. Sleep, unfortunately, was not an option for him. It was less so now than ever before.

But Charlie wouldn't be given any choice. He blinked once. He blinked twice. When he blinked again, he inexplicably found himself lying in his bed with the moonlight illuminating his frosty window. He wore his gray uniform now and not the pajamas he'd worn since he got up that morning.

"I can't have slept!" he said to himself. "I can't have! It's a trick!"

All the while, the winter wind screamed with thrice the fury of all the past nights, but Charlie heard one scream that was most certainly not made by the wind.

This scream was unquestionably from Georgie.

With all his might, Charlie tried to force open the window, but it was frozen fast.

"I hate this stupid house!" he shouted, and he slammed his hand against the glass. A funny thing, though: The pane didn't feel like glass at all. It felt, strangely, like paper. *What?* he thought. The window certainly looked real enough, and through the frost he could see the shadow of snowflakes collecting on the other side. Yet when Charlie poked the strange glass with his finger, the window actually tore, revealing only plain white wall behind it.

"Witch magic! I knew it!" he said to himself, but Charlie also knew there was no time to wonder at this mystery. His sister was somewhere out there in the cursed beyond, and time to find her was surely running out.

Charlie leaped from his bed and raced across the room for the door. Just as he feared, it was locked from the outside.

"Oh no you don't!" he shouted at the house, Grandmother Pearl, the so-called hired men—whoever and whatever might hear him. "You thought you could get past me because I'm a coward, but now you've gone and crossed the line!"

Charlie grabbed the door handle again and squeezed it until it felt as hot as his anger. For just a moment, the door seemed to be one with his arm as a force heretofore unknown to him traveled from his chest and out through his hand.

"Open up!" he shouted. There was the sound of clicking and whirring from within, and then, to Charlie's natural surprise and alarm, the door unlocked and flung free of his hand, swinging as wide open as Charlie's mouth. And who should be waiting for him in the hallway? None other than the white cat with the cold, staring eyes. Talos arched his back and hissed, his icy blue eyes now huge black marbles, his bared fangs too long and too many.

"You!" Charlie spat. Talos growled in reply and swiped at his ankle, drawing four red ribbons of blood, but Charlie had no time to tussle with ill-tempered house cats, not even enchanted ones. Ignoring the beast, he leaped through the door and ran as fast as he could without looking back.

But the more he ran, the longer the hall seemed to grow. *The house knows,* he thought, but he kept going. *Where are the grandmothers?* he wondered. Surely Grandmother Pearl would have stopped him by now. If he ran into Grandmother Opal, would she help him, or was she a slave to her wicked sister? There were too many things that could go wrong, and there wasn't a moment to waste thinking about any of them. In his mind, Charlie pictured the front door of the house, knowing that if he kept his thoughts on the destination and not the perils of the journey, he could sustain his courage.

But the house *did* know what he intended to do, and the house had other plans. In the blink of an eye, the opening before him terminated in a wall that hadn't been there before.

"No! This is a bad dream!" Charlie cried, but in his thundering heart, he knew it was real. The pain where Talos had scratched him served as violent proof of that. He pushed on all the same, turning down one corner and then another. Nothing took him where he needed to go, and he sensed that Talos would give him more trouble soon.

Then he thought of something.

"I'm hungry, and I want to go to the kitchen!" Charlie announced, feeling a bit silly for talking to a house. *Think about the kitchen. Don't think about anything else. The kitchen. The kitchen. The kitchen!*

It must have worked, for the next turn Charlie took opened out into the parlor he knew. He took one look at the kitchen doorway and then spun 180 degrees, racing for the front door before the house and its magic could catch on to his plan. This door opened easily, and Charlie's legs carried him outside faster than he dared think possible.

Once he was on the porch, however, his resolve all but died.

"Not now! You *can't* be scared now!" he scolded himself, but the voice inside his thoughts said the very opposite. *You'll just get yourself killed, and you won't have saved anyone. None of this is really happening anyway. You've probably just misunderstood, and Georgie's safe and sound inside.*

"No! Keep going!" Charlie ordered himself.

Just ahead of the porch, that foul and familiar fog gathered again. In it, something moved. This something was small and black and hard to see clearly, and from the center of it a light beamed brightly. The light wavered as if the object reflecting it were twisting and turning in slow motion, bouncing back the glow of the moon ten times brighter than the moon actually was.

"You again!" Charlie said to the black cat, but just as before—just as *always*—the cat turned tail and scampered away.

"I'm supposed to follow you, aren't I?" Charlie asked, squinting in the fog. He sighed with frustration then and muttered, "I ought to call you Mister Gordon after my Latin teacher. I can never keep up with him, either."

Charlie could just barely make out the shape of the animal and the light reflecting from whatever ornament it wore. Charlie chased it around the side of the house twice and then back twice more in the other direction until the cat stopped before a small door.

"Georgie's door!" Charlie exclaimed, yet when he looked for the mysterious black cat, it was gone.

"Wait!" Charlie called out into the fog. "Come back, Mister Gordon! Is this where Georgie is? Is this where they've taken my sister?"

But Charlie was alone. Truly alone, it appeared, for a quick glance around revealed no sign of either Talos or the grandmothers emerging from that evil mist, and they were never far behind. Charlie wasn't sure he liked the ease of this rescue mission so far. Suspicious, it was. Highly suspicious.

It wasn't as if he had much choice, however, so he stooped and pulled hard at the curious little door. He had expected that it wouldn't budge; it had been locked when Georgie tried before. But to Charlie's simultaneous gladness and suspicion, it gave him no trouble at all. He peered into the opening and saw nothing but darkness and a barely visible ladder going down, down into the black.

Well, this is it, he told himself. *Whether you lose your nerve or not, you're in big trouble now. You might as well go on.*

With a gulp and an awful sinking feeling in his belly, Charlie descended the ladder into the depths until his feet landed upon a flat surface. Far above him, the little doorway was a tiny square of dim light. Below him were stairs. How many, he couldn't guess without any light to see by. He could only feel blindly along the cold, damp walls and hope he didn't stumble.

It felt like those stairs went on forever. Down and down, down to the center of the earth perhaps. Far deeper than any fruit cellar would. After quite a long time, Charlie saw a faint light somewhere below, and it grew steadily brighter the more he descended. He heard noises, too: voices and metal clanking and sounds he couldn't identify that grew louder as he drew close.

After a terribly long walk, Charlie reached the bottom. The air reeked of sulfur here. A single torch lit a narrow arched entrance, but its flame offered no warmth. As if anything could have warmed him with the danger he knew he faced now. He held his breath and flattened himself against the wall. Then he swallowed hard and slowly peeked around the corner, praying that nothing would catch him. What he saw horrified him to his very core.

Ahead of him was a huge cave, with more torches casting dim light over the horrible dealings within. Children of all ages gathered by the thousands in a great hall. All of them wore gray uniforms just like Georgie's and his own, and every child was bound by chains and manacles that were in turn connected to one long chain, which kept them all together. *So this was what they planned for us!* Charlie thought. He scanned the crowd for signs of his sister, but he was too far away to make out any faces clearly.

The torchlight illuminated even greater horrors, for stalking the cave were creatures like nothing Charlie had seen before, even in the worst of his dreams. Some he saw were tall and gaunt. Others more squat and blubbery. All had hairless, gray skin that was slick with slime and studded with warts, and from his vantage it appeared they had only holes for eyes. They paced the hall, these monsters, prodding at the children with long fingers that looked like pale tarantula legs and growling orders in the same harsh voices Charlie had once been told belonged to "hired men."

And the uniforms of these hideous fiends were ill-fitting dresses, Charlie saw with sickening dread. Grandmotherly dresses.

One such creature, who wore a garish floral gown and a string of pearls, stood at a dais before the corral of children and seemed to be performing as a judge of sorts. "What is your name?" she asked as a small girl was unchained from the others and brought forward. This child was tiny with wispy blond hair, and she could not have been more than five years old.

"Your name, child! What is it?" demanded the judge again.

The child stuttered, "I d-don't remember!"

"Who were your parents?" asked the judge.

"Please, sir or ma'am, I can't recall if I have any!" squeaked the child.

The judge nodded approvingly. "This one is ready. She shall be called Kettle Tarnish, and she goes to the weaving room," she announced. "Next! What is your name?"

On went the process for countless children. None remembered so much as his or her own name, and all were sent away to different caverns after strange new names were assigned them by their slimy masters. Stinky Foot to the hammering hall, Soot Broom to the kitchen, Stubborn Hangnail to the garden of refuse, and so on.

Until one child *did* remember.

"What is your name?" asked the judge, scratching at a wart on her chin.

"Al-al-alex, please," said a boy.

"ALEX?"

"M-my parents are James and Marybeth. They're schoolteachers. W-w-we live in East Gingham."

"THIS ONE REMEMBERS!" boomed the creature, to the roaring rage (or was it delight?) of the other monsters. "FEED HIM TO THE PHANTOMS!"

Charlie watched as the poor frightened Alex was led away to some unseen chamber while the creatures all cackled like jackals. Then something took hold of Charlie's hair and pulled him backward into the shadows.

"My, my! It seems we have ourselves a snooper, doesn't it?" said someone in Grandmother Opal's voice, but the face Charlie saw before him was nothing human. It wore Grandmother Opal's dress on its deformed frame, and it sported her familiar black ring on one of its spider-leg fingers. Beyond this, however, it bore no resemblance.

"Grandmother Opal?!" Charlie sputtered.

"That's right, dear," said the Grandmother Opal creature, but no longer in the kindly voice Charlie knew. Now she spoke with as gruff and deep a tone as the other monsters he had seen in the cavern full of children.

Lurking just behind Grandmother Opal and standing a good two feet taller was a different sort of creature entirely. This one wore no clothes at all, save for a thick metal collar. Apart from this, it was all bones and sagging skin with awkwardly long limbs that ended in webbed claws. It had a pair of icy blue eyes, a mouth full of sharp teeth, and long white fur that trailed from its otherwise bald head all the way down its bony spine in one long streak. The creature may have stood upright like a man, but Charlie saw something grotesquely catlike about its face.

"Talos . . . ," Charlie murmured.

The monster that had once been Grandmother Opal barked out a laugh. "There! Now you've got the idea!" she said before she ordered the other creature, "Bring me Grandmother Pearl!"

Talos wordlessly stalked around Charlie and soon returned with another monster like Grandmother Opal, only this one wore Grandmother Pearl's high-collared gown and cameo brooch. Charlie's breath caught in his throat at the sight of her. Her face—if one would even call it such—was badly bruised. Something like blood but dark and green seeped from cuts above one of her eyes and below her jutting cheekbones.

"Yes, General," sniveled the one who was Grandmother Pearl, cowering before the other.

"You see why I had to punish you," said Grandmother Opal. "You were charged with keeping the children away from our operations until the appropriate time, and your repeated negligence has led this one to find us far too soon! What should I do with you, Grandmother Pearl?"

"Destroy me, Most High General Grandmother. I have failed you and Her Majesty," said Grandmother Pearl through clenched teeth.

"And so I shall," said Grandmother Opal. She held out one hand with the black ring facing the subordinate grandmother, and from the ring beamed a streak of pure shadow. The condemned yelped once and then promptly vanished.

Charlie felt sick to his stomach. *It's too real to be a nightmare, but it's too horrible to be real,* he thought. *How am I going to get out of this?* His thoughts were interrupted when Grandmother Opal grabbed him by his collar and pulled him close to her disgusting face.

"Now that you've seen us in our true form, child," she said, her foul breath pervading Charlie's nose, "why don't you tell us your name?"

CHAPTER SIX

THE STUFF OF NIGHTMARES

This was the moment that had consumed Charlie's nightmares for half his twelve years. The darkness he had long sensed would swallow up his family, the monster that would seize everyone he loved—it had come at last. And oh, how swiftly had its work been done! It had sickened Mother and swept Georgie away, just as it had taken every other child he knew—and in a matter of days. *But,* said a voice in the back of Charlie's mind, the voice that had always been muffled by too many worries before, *it's not too late.* He'd never had the courage to fight, but what had been the point of his many fears if not this? There was nothing left. All the fear in the world had been used up, and it hadn't done him a whit of good.

"Your name, child! Out with it!" snarled Grandmother Opal, tightening her grip on Charlie's shirt collar. Her breath stank of brimstone and the slime that grows on rotten ham.

At first Charlie didn't understand. Grandmother Opal knew

him. Why would she ask for his name? But then Charlie remembered the fate of the unfortunate Alex. He didn't know what the "phantoms" were, but he had no intention of being fed to them or to anything else.

"Thomas!" he declared. "No. No, it's William, isn't it?"

Grandmother Opal grinned, her mouth a yellow crescent moon, and Charlie knew he'd answered well.

"You tell *me*," Grandmother Opal said, her grin growing wider.

"I don't know," Charlie lied, "but please don't be angry! I'll try harder to remember! No, it's Nicholas! It must be Nicholas!"

When Grandmother Opal laughed, she sounded like a barking baboon. She was clearly pleased, but Charlie knew he had to maintain the act if he wanted to get any closer to reuniting his family.

"And how did you come to find yourself down here, Thomas-William-No-It's-Nicholas?" Grandmother Opal asked him.

Charlie had to think quickly on this one. "I was trying to sort out where I was," he pretended, though his trembling was very real. "All I could remember is that I had a pair of grandmothers, but I couldn't find either one to help me. I opened all the doors I could, and then I—I—I got lost outside. Am I in trouble?"

Grandmother Opal didn't answer him and instead addressed the silent Talos. "I honestly thought this one couldn't be brought over," she said, "but perhaps you didn't fail me after all. He's turned out far better than I could have hoped. Yes, even better than his wayward nuisance of a sister!"

The monster's words angered Charlie, but showing it would bring about his and almost certainly Georgie's demise. Instead, he put all his efforts into looking exactly as confused as he felt.

"What's the matter, boy? Don't remember your sister?" taunted Grandmother Opal in her old voice again. It was so much worse than her natural voice now that Charlie knew it was full of lies.

"Not to worry, dear," she said, fishing a pair of manacles out of her dress pocket. "She doesn't remember you, either."

Click! went the manacles onto Charlie's wrists, and *crack!* went his heart. Then Talos gave him a shove, and Charlie went marching into the great hall with Grandmother Opal accompanying him. Charlie looked at the faces of the other prisoners as he passed them. All of them looked back at him sorrowfully, and none that he could see was Georgie. *Good heavens,* Charlie thought. *All of them once thought they were going to visit their grandmothers!*

"STOP!" boomed the creature at the dais. "Explain this newcomer!"

"It is a boy, Your Honor! An older one but still valuable," Grandmother Opal called back in answer.

"Why haven't you put him in with the others?" asked the judge.

"I have already questioned him and found him viable," answered Grandmother Opal. "I recommend him for immediate placement in the figment chamber."

The other children softly gasped, and Charlie saw that some shook their heads. But the judge sniffed the air with her gray carrot of a nose and grimaced.

"No," she decided with a shake of her horrible head. "Too fresh! This one will be called Mousetrap. Deliver him to the kitchen! And, General, I expect all newcomers henceforth to be placed in line for proper processing. No more exceptions!"

"Of course, Your Honor. It was my mistake," said Grandmother

Opal with a sneer. Then she bowed her head and stepped back into the shadows. If Charlie never saw her again, it would've been too soon.

He took one last searching glance for his sister as Talos pulled him away. But among so many captives and without time to look more carefully, any hope of finding Georgie in that crowd was as good as trying to hold on to a kite in a hurricane. And if any of the monsters should catch on that he knew whom he'd lost, Charlie would never have the chance to look again.

Besides, he remembered painfully, how could he convince Georgie to flee with him if he did manage to break free and find her? If Grandmother Opal was right, his sister didn't know him anymore. This was going to be harder than Charlie had expected when he first climbed down that cellar ladder, and it was going to take two things of which he had very little: time and nerve.

The place the grandmothers called the "kitchen" was another cavern, this one marked with stalactites that hung from its ceiling and dripped slime. Beneath these formations were huge black machines of all sorts, their numerous cogs and wheels grinding like teeth as steam belched out of narrow towers all throughout the chamber. It was as hot and miserable as perdition in that kitchen. Charlie wondered if any place in this underground labyrinth could possibly be worse, and then he silently chastised himself for inviting the answer.

On the floor before the machines stood vats twelve feet high and full of something that bubbled and stank, each one stirred by a different child. Every worker, even the tallest of them, had to stand tippy-toed on rickety ladders to reach the handles of their giant stirring spoons. It was here that Talos released Charlie and unchained his wrists without a word. A short and fat monster in a blue dress waddled over to Charlie then and shoved a grimy apron into his hands.

"You!" she said with a disdainful snort. "Put that on. You get any soup on you before it's done, and it'll eat you 'fore *you* can eat *it*. Heh heh! *And hurry up.*"

Charlie quickly threw the apron on and was just tying the strings when the fat little creature began pushing him over to a freckle-faced boy with orange hair who looked to be about Charlie's age.

"What's your name again, boy?" the monster asked the other.

"Ch-chicken Liver, Grandmother Jewel," the boy stuttered without looking up from his bare feet.

Grandmother Jewel guffawed and addressed Charlie. "Ch-ch-ch-chicken Liver will show you how to do the doings around here," she said, "and I'm the one who'll be keeping an eye on you, so no funny business!"

She reached into one of her eyeholes and pulled out a shiny black eyeball, which she let go with a snap back into its place deep within her scummy face. Then she cackled and waddled away. If Charlie hadn't already seen worse that very night, he might have lost his lunch. *I suppose that's a sort of progress,* he thought to cheer himself up. It didn't help.

"Come on. My station is this way," said the freckle-faced boy, calmer now that Grandmother Jewel wasn't around. "What do they call you anyway?"

"Char—er, Mousetrap," answered Charlie.

"Mind that you watch your stirring, Mousetrap," said Chicken Liver, climbing up a ladder beside a particularly steamy vat. "Do what I do and always stir counterclockwise. Not too fast, but not too slow, neither, or it'll eat the spoon."

Charlie climbed another ladder and peered into the soup. It was oily and black and most certainly the source of the sulfury odor he'd smelled before.

"What *is* this?" he asked.

"It's tomorrow's meal for all of us," Chicken Liver replied. "It's easier if you pour it right down your throat and skip the tongue."

Charlie felt himself on the verge of gagging and decided he'd rather not know what the soup was actually made of.

"What happens if I stir it the wrong way?" he asked.

"You'll ruin it," said Chicken Liver as he hefted a wooden spoon from a hook on the outside of the vat, "and if you ruin it, we'll *all* be in trouble."

Charlie watched as Chicken Liver stood on his toes and leaned over the side of the vat, holding the great spoon handle with both hands to stir the muck. Though the soup was as black as tar, it somehow bathed the other boy in a green light. Charlie now wished he'd eaten more of the awful food at the house before he'd come here. It was always burnt or greasy or put together all wrong, but at least none of it glowed. Unfortunately, he'd never eaten much of it, and he wasn't sure how long he could hold out without eating now.

"There. I've shown you how it works," said Chicken Liver. "Your station's right next to mine. Remember: Always stir counterclockwise! Not too fast and not too slow. At the end of the day, I'll show you how to drain the soup into the proper containers and clean the empty vat."

Charlie nodded and carefully made his way down that ladder and then up the unmanned vat beside Chicken Liver's. He took a spoon just like the freckled boy had shown him and stirred counterclockwise. Whenever he thought no one was looking—which was difficult, as Grandmother Jewel was forever pacing around the chamber—he surveyed the kitchen for signs of his sister. Again there was nothing.

"Chicken Liver!" he hissed after the grandmother's latest round. The other boy glanced at him out of the side of his eye but made no other acknowledgment. *Probably too scared*, Charlie thought, but he took his chances and tried again. "Chicken Liver! Over here!"

Chicken Liver looked to his left, then to his right, and then answered Charlie.

"What is it now?" he asked, and not without irritation.

"Have you ever heard of a girl named Georgie?" asked Charlie.

Chicken Liver went quite pale for a second and immediately resumed his stirring. Grandmother Jewel came around again, stopped, and squinted at the two boys. Then she harrumphed and went on her way.

"It doesn't sound like any name I've heard down here," said the freckle-faced boy.

Of course! Charlie thought. *They'd have given her a new name!*

"She's eight, and she's small with curly brown hair," Charlie described. "She would've gotten here shortly before me."

But Chicken Liver shook his head once and focused on his work. It was clear to Charlie that he wouldn't be getting any more information out of the freckle-faced boy.

Another grandmother came in to deliver something to Grandmother Jewel. This one stopped, studied Charlie for a moment, and then went on her way.

"Psst!" someone whispered.

Charlie looked all around until he saw a tall girl waving at him from the vat just across from his. When they met eyes, the girl pretended to drop her spoon on the ground. As she went to fetch another, she stopped at Charlie's ladder.

"If she's small, she'd probably be in the weaving room," said the girl without looking at him, "unless she's been sent straight to the figment chamber, poor thing."

"What's the figment chamber?" Charlie asked, but the girl was already on her way back to her station.

It was Chicken Liver who spoke up this time. "We aren't supposed to remember anyone from *before*," he said in a hushed voice. "If you remember someone, especially someone down here, then you'd best forget her. It would be better for everyone."

But Charlie had so many questions to ask! Why were they made to forget their families? Why did *he* remember when they didn't? Who—no, *what*—were the grandmothers, and why were they stealing children to do their work? What and why and who and how—it didn't matter what he asked, for no one would talk to him.

Suddenly, there was a pop and a hiss, and Charlie saw that his soup was about to boil over. There were green swirls disrupting the black surface of the tarry soup, but the smell was weirdly like roses. Charlie looked up to find the other soup-stirrers glaring at him.

"Are you some kind of half-wit?" snapped Chicken Liver. "You're stirring the wrong way!"

Charlie realized he had been stirring clockwise for the past five minutes instead of counterclockwise and, panicking, he dropped the spoon into the soup.

"Oh no!" he said.

"Now you've done it!" someone grumbled.

The soup stopped swirling and issued a puff of steam before absorbing the utensil completely. The spoon sizzled and smoked as it dissolved, and the smoke itself sparked, which ignited the very air around it in plumes of flame that engulfed the stalactite above. This fire would surely have spread had the grandmother known as Jewel not extinguished it with the power of a ring identical to Grandmother Opal's.

"MOUSETRAAAAAAAAP!" she roared, and Charlie cringed. He shivered. He thought words he daren't say in polite company.

Charlie wasn't allowed to remain long enough to see if the other kitchen children were punished on account of his clumsiness. He was whisked away by more guards—guards with hairless, cat-like faces similar to Talos's—before he could so much as say he was sorry. That filthy apron was torn from him, he was clasped in irons again, and he was led down corridors that twisted and turned until he heard the terrible commotion of crashing and banging and crunching glass. Inside a new chamber, he saw mountains of glittering, broken objects, which more uniformed children were smashing into smaller bits with hammers bigger than their heads.

Charlie's heart sank as he saw what those objects were. Alarm clocks. Gobs of them. He thought of his own missing clock and felt that little prickly feeling in his eyes again, but he would not cry. Not over this. All the clocks in the world could not tick his family back together anyway, and that was what he had to remember.

One of the guards quietly removed Charlie's shackles, handed him a pair of work boots to replace his flimsy slippers, and placed a hammer in his hands.

"This is the hammering hall!" announced Grandmother Jewel, and with a grunt she added, "Since you're positively *exquisite* at ruining things, you ought to have no trouble here."

She exited, and Charlie was left among the piles of broken clocks and all the workers who were forced to destroy them. At the head of this cavern of destruction was a grandmother who stood tall and thin like a broom handle. She hadn't noticed Charlie yet, for which he was grateful.

"Smash them!" she ordered the workers in a high-pitched screech unlike the deep bellow of most other grandmothers. "Shatter them! Demolish every cog and wheel!"

She marched between the piles and grabbed a girl by the chin.

"And *why* do we destroy?" she asked the girl, who mumbled something Charlie couldn't hear. The grandmother shrilled, "Louder, child, louder! *Why* do we destroy?"

"Her Majesty despises a working clock, Grandmother Ruby!" the girl repeated loudly.

"Excellent," the grandmother replied. "And why does she despise a working clock?"

"Because it weakens the dreams by which she takes flight, Grandmother Ruby!"

"Good. Never forget it," said Grandmother Ruby, and she went back to her violent chants, clapping her hands together with each phrase.

"Shatter them! Demolish them! Annihilate time itself!"

Not wishing to attract any attention by simply standing there slack-jawed, Charlie fell in with a smaller group of workers at the back and heaved his hammer over his head exactly as they did. The weight of it was inconceivable. Sweat poured down his face upon the very first lift. And yet the other children swung their tools with an ease that one could describe as graceful. Even the clock fragments that tumbled through the air did so in unnaturally slow motion, torchlight bouncing off each glittering shard, turning detritus into diamonds as the pieces hung in the air for just a moment before falling. It would have been beautiful had it not been so *weird*, and had it not meant what it did. Indeed, it crushed Charlie's soul a little bit with every strike, and for once, he was grateful for those imaginary heart chains that kept his feelings in check. It would do no good to show any attachment to anything now.

But each time Charlie raised that giant hammer, he took the chance to scan the cavern for his sister. And each time he looked, he was met with only discouragement. If everything the kitchen girl had said was true, though, Georgie would be too small to work in the hammering hall. "The weaving room," the girl had said. That was where his sister was likely to be. Not here. The thought gave Charlie comfort, but what a paltry comfort it was. However was he to get to the weaving room?

"Hey," he said to the worker beside him, a tall, broad-shouldered boy with sandy hair and an upturned nose. "I'm Mousetrap."

The boy was startled but muttered quickly, "Milkweed."

Smash! Crash! Bang! went the hammering all around them. There was a pattern to it, Charlie noticed, almost like song.

"Can you tell me something, Milkweed?" Charlie asked the tall boy.

"Probably not."

Crush! Crunch! Shatter! Another verse in destruction.

"What's the weaving room, and where is it?"

Milkweed only shrugged and kept at his smashing and crashing. Charlie was crestfallen. It was no use. No one would answer his questions. They all either were too afraid or had been kept too long in the dark. He would have to find another way to get his answers. Perhaps, he thought, he could hide himself in the shuffle and work his way from chamber to chamber until he found the weavers. There were so very many prisoners here that there was no possible way the grandmothers could account for them all. But when? Would he ever get the chance to leave this cavern?

The answer came with the earsplitting clang of a gong.

"Sleep time! Fall in line for the time of sleeping!" barked Grandmother Ruby.

Bedtime? Charlie thought. *Can daylight have come and gone so soon?* Ah, but Grandmother Opal and Grandmother Pearl had kept

strange sleeping schedules themselves. They were always napping in the morning, Charlie remembered, and he could never find them at night. He wondered if that meant it was really morning now. Whatever the time, he saw an opportunity. If all the children were being moved, this could be his chance to slip into another group without anyone catching on.

But discouragement met him yet again. The children were once more shackled to one another, making easy escape out of the question. Soon after, Charlie and the others were marched in lines down one narrow corridor until they reached the enormous cavern in which all of them were meant to sleep. It was like a small city, this place—a city of towers made up of bunk beds. There, each child was unchained from the line and directed to an assigned bed.

Charlie's own bunk was second from the top of the biggest stack of beds he'd ever heard of. Flashes of falling and broken bones rushed to the stage of his thoughts, but he wasn't about to ask for a bed lower to the ground. *Besides,* he told himself, *the higher up I am, the easier it will be to look for Georgie.* But the elevation of his bed made the search no simpler than any previous attempt. There were simply too many children and too many bed towers blocking his sight.

Once all the children lay in their beds, the grandmothers and their guards departed to their own quarters. Charlie found this bewildering. The children were all so carefully guarded at other times. Why would the grandmothers trust a roomful of children to stay put and obey on their own? *There must be worse waiting for us if we try to get out,* he thought. No, he would not venture an escape.

He could not risk his sister's safety until he knew more. *But soon*, he thought. *Hold on, Georgie. Wherever you are, keep holding on.*

Charlie lay on his back and stared at the bottom of the bed above his. He closed his eyes and tried to imagine he was someplace else, but the squeak of bedsprings and the stench of sulfur made this impossible. Sometime after all the grandmothers had gone, there was a sound like a gentle breeze filtering through the room. Charlie opened his eyes and looked all around to discover that the breeze was the sound of all the children whispering to one another. *This must be their only chance,* he thought. He tried to listen in to find what he could learn, but there were too many voices to filter out.

"Hey!" whispered a voice right into his ear. Charlie jerked and looked up. Leaning out of the bunk across from his own was a small boy with shaggy brown hair.

"Hey," Charlie warily answered.

The other boy pushed himself a little closer. "There's a rumor going around," said the boy. "Kids are saying you remember something. Something from before you got here."

Charlie's stomach clenched, and he quickly shook his head. "No," he fibbed. "I don't remember anything. Must be someone else."

"Nah," said the brown-haired boy. "Nah, it was you. They said you had curly hair, and you were new. I know you haven't been here long. What's it like?"

"Well, it's horrible," said Charlie.

"No, not *this place*," said the boy. "Of course *this place* is horrible. I mean, what's it like to remember things?"

"I told you already. I don't remember anything."

"Hmm," said the other boy, withdrawing into his bunk. "Suit yourself."

Charlie tried to close his eyes again, but all the questions he wanted to ask were darting around his head. *That boy wanted to talk,* he thought. *So, maybe he knows things.* Charlie flopped onto his belly and leaned over the edge of his bed.

"Hey," he whispered. The brown-haired boy was immediately at attention again. Charlie asked him, "What's your name?"

"Badger Brush. I work in the kitchen," the other said eagerly, and he extended a grimy hand in greeting. "I saw you when you almost set the place on fire. You're Mousetrap, aren't you? Boy, does Chicken Liver have it in for *you*! He got put on double duty for not catching you before ol' Grandma Jewel did."

Charlie avoided confirming anything and instead asked, "What is this place? Why have they done this to us?"

Badger Brush propped himself up on his elbows. "You ever imagine anything?" he asked.

"Huh?" said Charlie.

"You know. Imagine things. Make pictures in your head. Think."

"Of course I do."

"This, kid, is a mine," said Badger Brush, gesturing to the cave around them, "and those ugly ladies who call themselves our grandmothers are the miners. What they're after is the dream stuff in our heads, see? The jelly that makes the pictures you think up. They need it for some reason. I don't know what for. So they made themselves up like they were grandmothers to get us to trust them. 'Cuz what kid doesn't love his grandma, right? Now, I don't remember anything from before. How do I know if I even had a real grand-mother? Well, I don't anymore. *That's* how they get you."

"That doesn't make any sense," said Charlie.

"I'm telling it true!" insisted Badger Brush. "They took our memories away so we'd be easier to mine. To *harvest*, they call it. But they're so good at it that they have more of the dream stuff than they need. In the meantime, they make us work until they need more. Somebody's got to keep the whole factory in order, after all."

"Is that what the figment chamber is for?" asked Charlie. "To harvest the . . . the jelly?"

"That's what I think. Nobody really knows for sure except the kids who get taken there," said Badger Brush, "but the kids who get taken there . . ."

"Yes?"

"They never come back."

Charlie pulled his flimsy sheet closer. Badger Brush seemed the type to delight in tall tales. But there was a time when Charlie would never have thought up the very monsters that imprisoned him here. What reason did he have to doubt?

"Don't you remember anything from before? Anything at all?" Charlie asked his new friend.

Badger Brush shook his head. "I remember that things weren't always like this," he said, "but the rest is just dandelion fluff. Sometimes I think I remember something, but just when I think I've got ahold of it—*poof!*—nothing but scattered fuzz.

"That's not the worst thing, though," he continued. "The worst is the Queen. I only saw her from a distance once, but she scared me so bad I nearly cried. And I'm telling you, kid, I'm no baby!"

"Who is this queen?" asked Charlie.

"That I don't know," said Badger Brush. "All *I* know is—"

Badger Brush fell abruptly silent. He turned his head, listened, and then paled. *"Bedbugs!"* he gasped.

"What?" said Charlie.

"Hush!" whispered Badger Brush.

Charlie listened, too. The whispering throughout the room had come to a halt. The other children were diving under bedclothes or pulling their pillows over their heads. Then Charlie heard a very different sort of whispering. It sounded like a breeze rushing through the trees. It was a whispering he would soon discover was made by a million tiny legs skittering across the cavern floor.

"Stay absolutely still and keep your ears covered!" Badger Brush instructed. "Whatever you do, *don't let them bite you!*"

Charlie quickly did as he was told, squeezing the pillow around his ears so tightly he could scarcely hear a thing beyond his own pulse in his ears. But from under that pillow, he saw what visited the children in their beds. He saw the bedbugs.

There were thousands upon thousands of them, and they covered the floor like a glittering black carpet. They resembled the beetles that Charlie had seen in books about far-off tropical countries. Most were the size of a baby's hand, but some here and there were as big as grown cats. The monstrous insects swept across the floor and then over the children, too, blanketing each one as they passed. Charlie watched, petrified, as some of those vile bedbugs wriggled their enormous selves into the ears of unlucky souls who had not been warned as he had. He closed his eyes to block out the horror, praying with every hope that these devil bugs would pass him by.

But they were coming closer. Closer and closer! Charlie's pillow could not muffle their legs *click-click-click*ing upon every surface. He listened with terror as they crawled up the posts of his very bunk tower. Up one bed. Then another. Another yet. And then they were upon his. Soon, they were crawling across his sheet, over his feet, his legs, his back. There were so many they utterly covered him. And as they drew near his head, he thought he heard the tiniest of voices chanting all together: *Yes, kiddies, yes! Tell us all your thoughtsy-thoughts! Tell us, tell us, TELL US!*

I forgot to hide my hands! Charlie thought with a great panic, but he knew that if he tried to do so now, his movement might just inspire the insects to bite, and he didn't know what their bites would do. How they tickled as they marched across his fingers!

But Charlie was fortunate, for the bedbugs moved on. Eventually, the sounds of their horrible little legs and their horrible little voices quieted and died, and there was silence throughout the sleeping hall. Nary a whisper could be heard. Not even Badger Brush dared stir.

Charlie thought he would be sick. Those tiny voices had sounded startlingly familiar. Like the voice he once overheard urging Mother to send Georgie and him away. The words of the rag-and-bone woman replayed in his mind now. *The buggies march in two by two, and they make little puppets o' me and you!* But that had just been the nonsense of a madwoman. She couldn't possibly have had any

connection to all this. She couldn't have been trying to tell him something that he foolishly ignored. . . .

That's not doing any good. Keep calm! You have to! For Georgie and Mother! he told himself. There was a lullaby that Father used to sing to him, he remembered, and though he had been very small then, he still recalled how it always made the worst of things seem all right.

Sleep, my little Charlie boy, it went. *Just close your eyes and rest.*
Dream of circus elephants and monkeys in red vests.
Charlie, don't you worry. Don't you cry, no, not a peep!
I'll make all the monsters promise they will let you sleep.

But with no one to sing the monsters away now, sleep was the very last thing Charlie could do. No, he would have to stay awake. *Stay awake,* he thought, *and be brave.*

CHAPTER SEVEN

PIGEON

The new day began with the clang of a gong and some grand-mother's ugly bark of "Get up! Time for your feeding, kiddies! Is there dust in your ears? I said *up!*"

Charlie hadn't slept for even a moment, but the others were rudely awakened by grandmothers shouting and rapping on the frames of the bunks with iron rods.

"What do we do?" Charlie whispered to Badger Brush. Badger Brush pantomimed eating.

"Oh," Charlie whispered. The *feeding.* That meant it was time to eat the nasty black sludge he had nearly wrecked only the day before. How, he pondered, was he going to get out of this one, and should he even try? It was a miracle he was on his feet as it was. Many days had passed since he'd gotten any real sleep, and he needed to keep up his strength if he wanted to accomplish anything resembling a rescue.

What if the sludge is poison? he thought, and then, *No, it couldn't be!* The children here had been eating it for as long they had been captives in this place, he told himself. However long *that* might have been was a thought that unsettled Charlie immensely.

Once the children were awake and in their shoes, they were tethered together and led down to a mess hall, where the guards released them to sit on long, crudely carved benches before equally long tables. Over these hovered—in midair!—steaming black kettles of soup. Then the kettles dropped all at once with a thud upon each table's surface, signaling the beginning of the feeding time. Charlie watched with disgust as the children eagerly rushed to dip their humble bowls into the foul glop. How he longed for something so pleasant as burnt biscuits now!

He remembered the words of the ill-tempered kitchen boy, Chicken Liver. "It's easier if you pour it right down your throat and skip the tongue," he'd said. Charlie spooned the mess and watched as it hesitated before sliding off the spoon and plopping back into the bowl.

"You've got to eat, kid," said Badger Brush beside him. "Believe me, it's worse if you don't."

Badger Brush didn't bother with the spoon and instead tipped the bowl right into his mouth, swallowing the soup in one gulp.

"Ugh," said Charlie.

"Gotta eat it," said Badger Brush, wiping the goop from his face with his sleeve. "Might as well get it over with!"

Badger Brush's words were true; Charlie had no choice but to eat, and dwelling on the grossness of it all wasn't going to make it any easier for him. No matter how hard he tried to avoid tasting it, however, it wasn't completely possible. The food tasted exactly the way tar smelled. And yet whatever was in it, it was amazingly efficient. Charlie felt full after eating only half the meager bowl. *Better not force the rest*, he thought. *I'll just be sick.*

"Look here!" shouted a familiar voice. Charlie cringed as Grandmother Jewel approached.

"Little Prince Mousetrap doesn't think the food is good enough for him!" she said, at which the other grandmothers cackled. "Enjoy it, boy. It's the only meal you're getting today."

Charlie closed his eyes, gulped once, and then emptied the rest of the bowl, his eyes watering as he struggled to keep it from coming back up. Despite the manners Mother had instilled in him, however, he could not help himself, and he belched with unparalleled volume. He could see curls of green fog escape his lips! Grandmother Jewel nodded in satisfaction and then moved on to torment some other unfortunate soul while poor Charlie turned scarlet from shame.

"Don't let it get to you," whispered Badger Brush. "Happens to everyone the first time. I don't think I'd trust anybody who didn't let out a bone-shaker like that on their first day!"

As if to prove Badger Brush's point, another heinous burp erupted from elsewhere in the hall. If there were others, the noise of clattering bowls and spoons buried the sound. Clattering bowls and spoons, yes, but no *laughter*, and that bothered Charlie even more than his own embarrassment. In school, an eructation like that would have sent his classmates into hysterical giggling. He had always found such disruptions annoying back home. Here, however, it made him very sad. Here, everyone had forgotten how to be children.

Another jaw-rattling clang of the gong rang out, signaling the end of the daily feeding. And with a raucous cough, the judge in all her glaring floral fabric bellowed out her orders for the day.

"It is time for work!" she announced. "Each of you must return to your assigned group. Cooks! To the kitchen!"

"Back to the daily grind," said Badger Brush with a shrug, and he went off to join his workmates.

"Garbage sorters! To the garden! Weavers! To the weaving room! Get a move on, all of you!" shouted the judge.

The weavers! Charlie saw his chance and scrambled to fall in line with the batch of children heading off in the last direction the judge had pointed out. Ahead, he saw a girl, a smallish one with long, curly brown hair. His hopes soared. *Georgie!*

But his hopes were due to be dashed.

"Oh no you don't!" barked Grandmother Ruby. Exactly when she had approached, Charlie didn't know, but she grabbed him by the shoulder and pulled him back with bruising force. "Going the wrong way to the hammering hall, aren't you, *Mousetrap?*"

Charlie nodded quickly and hid his disappointment behind a mask of confusion. But as he turned to head back for his assigned work group, he looked one last time for his sister. Sadly, the long-haired girl he had caught sight of before was looking the other way, and her profile revealed she wasn't Georgie as he had hoped. Crushed, Charlie allowed himself to be shackled to his fellow hammerers and was led to where he belonged.

Though his arms ached terribly from the day before, Charlie did find his work easier this time. The hammer was only half as heavy to him now. Perhaps it was because he put his anger and fear and sadness into it as he swung. But as he did, he said his apologies to the alarm clock pieces he sent spiraling in a slow dance through the stagnant air.

"I'm sorry, little bells," he said. "I'm sorry, all you numbers. I'm sorry, cogs and wheels."

After a time, Charlie had the keen sense that he was being watched. Of course, Milkweed *pretended* to be preoccupied with his work, but Milkweed was proving to be terrible at pretending. He was most definitely watching Charlie out the corner of his eye, and so, Charlie noticed, were many of the other workers.

"What's wrong? Why's everyone staring?" Charlie asked, but Milkweed only kept up his shabby pretense of not hearing. Staring, however, wasn't the only thing Milkweed did a poor job of disguising. There was a pattern to his hammering again. *Bang! Crash! Swing! Tap-tap!* It was different from before, but it was distinctly there. What's more, Charlie heard answers to this pattern. From elsewhere in the room, three, four—maybe more—workers hammered out their reply in unison: *Tap-tap! Swing! Crunch! Bang!*

That's not just a rhythm. They're talking to each other! Charlie realized. It wasn't quite Morse code, but there was a system to it that he thought he could understand if only, like a cipher, he had the key. Why communicate this way, however, when everyone could talk almost freely at night? Charlie answered his own question as soon as he thought it: it was too easy, and nothing easy in this place could be trusted. How could anyone know they weren't being watched? And the bedbugs . . .

Charlie looked up to see if Grandmother Ruby was picking up on the rhythm the way he was. It seemed she was too involved in issuing motivational commands to hear anything but the sound of her own voice. So, Charlie took a chance. He swung his hammer around, and he banged out the exact same pattern Milkweed had sounded off moments ago. Then he lowered his hammer and waited, glaring.

Just as he expected, there were sharp looks in his direction from all over the hammering hall.

"What are you doing?" hissed Milkweed without looking at him.

"What does it mean?" Charlie asked defiantly.

"Grandmother Ruby will see us talking! Go back to your work before she catches us!"

"Tell me what it means, and I will."

Milkweed sighed and hammered out a little pattern that Charlie imagined to be some sort of warning to the others. *Hold on a minute,* maybe. Or, *Trouble here.*

Milkweed leaned in close, pretending to inspect a larger fragment of glass. "It's how we talk," he said.

"I figured out that much. So, what are you all saying? Translate a little," Charlie begged. "You know I'll figure it out eventually anyway." He *had* always been rather good at the cryptograms in the Sunday newspaper.

"I can't," Milkweed muttered.

"Why? Do you think I'm going to tell on you?" asked Charlie as he kicked around a small pile of cogs just for show.

"Maybe," said Milkweed.

"I would never!"

"You might think you won't, but they can *make* you, and sooner or later, they'll be onto you."

Charlie's pulse raced. "What do you mean they'll be *onto* me?" he asked.

Milkweed glanced at him sideways and then lifted his hammer high over his head. He banged out another pattern. It was loud and clear, and it was followed by numerous answers all over the hall.

"That?" said Milkweed. "That's about you. It means 'Rememberer.'"

Charlie gulped. "I don't know what you're talking about."

"Word spreads fast here, Mousetrap. You've been looking for someone," said Milkweed, "and if *we* know, it won't be long before *they* do. They'll turn you upside down and shake out everything you know, too. About us. About whomever it is you're trying to find. It's what they do."

Grandmother Ruby was approaching now, and there was a look of suspicion on her long, bony face. Charlie and Milkweed went back to their work silently, but Charlie's thoughts raced the whole time. Everyone knew, Milkweed had said. *I should've been more careful!*

"If I'm such bad news for you all, why haven't you turned me in yet?" Charlie said when Grandmother Ruby, satisfied that they were hard at work, left them alone.

"Because sometimes rememberers can do things the rest of us can't," Milkweed answered, "and we've been waiting a long time for a new rememberer."

"Waiting to do what?" asked Charlie.

"That's all I'm gonna say about it," said Milkweed. "I'm going back to work now. You ought to do the same."

Before Charlie could think about this much longer, the doors to the hammering hall were flung open, and in stepped a grandmother Charlie hadn't seen before. She brought with her a child whose features Charlie couldn't make out in the shadows. Quickly, the rhythm of hammering turned to chaos, and Charlie couldn't find the patterns anymore.

Grandmother Ruby and the other grandmother walked down between the work piles with the newcomer, talking. As they neared, Charlie pretended to focus on his work again lest it be seen that he was eavesdropping.

"I wouldn't normally take up your time with warnings about unruly children, Grandmother Ruby, but she is a handful!" said the other. "She makes knots in all the looms, and she does it on purpose! It's going to be days before we'll have any new dresses!"

"And why would you hand off such a troublemaker to me? She's barely big enough to hold a hammer," said Grandmother Ruby.

"She's stronger than you think. But there's not much havoc she can wreak in here," said the other. "And look at her! So much figment in that head of hers, you can smell it! But I wouldn't put her in for harvesting just yet. She's got too much willpower."

"I'll take care of that," said Grandmother Ruby.

She was right behind Charlie now, and after the conversation he'd just had with Milkweed, he was so nervous that his ears were sweating.

"Pick up a hammer, girl," Grandmother Ruby was saying to the newcomer. "Get to smashing! You won't be such a handful when you're too tired to lift your arms anymore."

The newcomer stood beside him now, but Charlie waited until Grandmother Ruby had left them to take a look at the small girl holding a hammer that was half her size. And when he did, his heart stopped.

It was Georgie.

Charlie's heart froze for only a moment, but it was a moment that nearly ruined everything. In that flash of an instant, the blood stopped traveling to his brain, and his brain didn't have the power to prevent him from blurting out what he thought.

"Georgie!" Charlie gasped. "You're alive!"

Luckily, no one important heard him through the sound of all those hammers. But Georgie heard him, and she glared, her face pale and thin, her long brown hair in a ratty tangle, her gray uniform much more tattered than anyone else's. *Of course it would be,* Charlie thought.

"What did you call me?" Georgie asked through her teeth.

"Don't you remember me? I'm Charlie! Your brother! I came here to get you out!" Charlie rambled. *Stupid thing to say!* he told himself, but he hadn't been able to help it.

Georgie snorted. "You're cuckoo. I don't have any brothers," she said. "I've been here for weeks, and no brothers or anyone else ever came looking for me, so why should I believe you? Now, leave me alone. I have work to do, and I can't get in trouble again."

With that, Georgie dragged her hammer to any clock pile where Charlie wasn't.

It occurred to Charlie then that time passed more quickly down here than it did aboveground. But the idea that the mere moments between Georgie's disappearance and Charlie's arrival could equal several weeks was simply beyond comprehension! He thought back to what Badger Brush had told him about the grandmothers and the "dream stuff." What sounded crazy then was sounding truer all the time.

But now Charlie had gone and upset his sister, which in turn upset him very much. He tried to console himself with the idea that he had at least found his sister alive. It was the best news he'd had since yesterday. Or was yesterday really only a few minutes ago in real-world time? The thought of it all made Charlie's head hurt more than it did already. He glanced Georgie's way and watched as she struggled to lift her heavy hammer.

How am I going to rescue someone who doesn't have the foggiest memory of who I am? he thought miserably. *If I can't save my own sister, how can I possibly be everyone else's rescuer, too? Milkweed is wrong. I'm not the rememberer they've been waiting for. I'm just a kid who lucked out, and for nothing.*

Meanwhile, Georgie attacked her workload with all the anger she must have felt in the many weeks she believed she'd been abandoned. *Please don't cause any trouble, Georgie!* Charlie silently pleaded. *This is your last chance. And it's my last chance to get us out of here!*

Then Georgie did a very strange thing. She dropped her hammer, stooped to inspect something, and then looked around twice before digging her hands in the rubbish pile and extracting an object her body blocked Charlie from seeing. Whatever it was, she slipped it into one of her uniform pockets, which were so large that the object in question made no defining shape. Suddenly, she glanced up at Charlie, caught him watching her, and scowled before she ran off to some other pile farther away.

"The time is for working, Mousetrap! Not for idleness!" screeched Grandmother Ruby, suddenly beside him.

"Yes, Grandmother Ruby," Charlie mumbled, and he threw himself back into his work, keeping his mind off his sore arms, the heartache, and the sheer misery of everything around him to think strictly on the challenge he knew lay ahead of him. In her right mind, Georgie would have seen this as a fantastic adventure. It certainly was an adventure. The most difficult adventure there had ever been.

But maintaining his focus became impossible when the hammering formed patterns again. They were scattered throughout the hall. He didn't know all the words, but he did recognize one repeated among his fellow laborers. Over and over and over they pounded it out, eyes on him. *REMEMBERER!* they said with their implements of destruction. *REMEMBERER! REMEMBERER! REMEMBERER!*

"It's going to be a good morning. Want to know how I know?" asked Badger Brush, lying on his belly and playing with a small dragon he'd fashioned out of pillow stuffing.

"How could it possibly be a good morning?" asked Charlie, who wasn't quite used to the idea that morning was bedtime now.

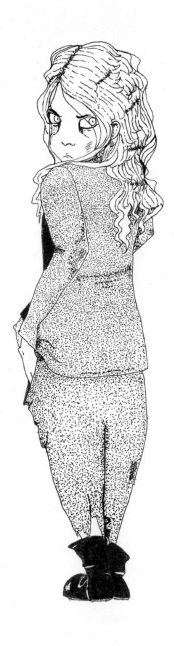

"The bedbugs won't come today!" said Badger Brush.

This gave Charlie pause, and he asked, "How do you know?"

"Stick around as long as me," answered Badger Brush, "and you start to pick things up."

"Stop trying to sound like an ol' wise owl," said a girl's voice. A head popped out from the bunk below Charlie's—a small girl with her dark hair in a messy bob. Her name, she said, was Horseshoe, and she worked in the weaving room, weaving fabric for the grandmothers' dresses on a giant loom alongside hundreds of other small children. They made the uniforms for the workers, too. Clothing just wasn't something the grandmothers were very good at producing on their own; they always got the finer details wrong.

"No one really knows when the bedbugs will come, but they rarely ever come two days in a row," Horseshoe explained with a roll of her eyes. "Their little buggy bellies get full of all the thoughts they steal from us, and they have to digest them. At least, that's my theory. Nobody can be sure. Not even Badger knows, smart as he tries to sound."

Badger Brush harrumphed. "Is that so? How long've *you* been here, Horseshoe? Not many can say they've been around as long as *I* have without getting harvested, and that takes smarts."

"You know how to hide, I'll give you that," conceded Horseshoe.

"It's all about the art of creating a good diversion," boasted Badger Brush.

"Wait a minute, hold on, go back a tick," said Charlie. "You say the bedbugs steal our thoughts?"

"Yeah, and sometimes they put new thoughts in," answered Badger Brush.

"If they can get into your head at all," Horseshoe added, "but

128

there's always some blockhead who forgets to cover up or squirms too much and gets bitten."

"Poor Mopsy," sighed Badger Brush.

"Mop Bucket was the best friend I had in this place before the bugs bit her," Horseshoe sadly explained. "They poisoned her and made her into a spy for them. But I knew something was wrong. You can usually tell when a kid's been bitten. They aren't themselves anymore. They're just a puppet."

"What happened to Mop Bucket after that?" Charlie asked.

Horseshoe's lip quivered for a moment, but in the end, she merely shrugged. Still, it was answer enough for Charlie. The sadness made the trio quiet, and before long, each was back in bed, attempting sleep. The other children in the city of bunks began to drop off into slumber as well, the day's labor making them too weary to take advantage of this holiday from the six-legged stalkers who threatened the sanctity of their own musings.

All except Charlie, of course, whose eyes were closed but whose brain was as busy as the weavers on their looms. *The bugs take thoughts out, and they put thoughts in,* he reasoned. So that's *how they got to Mother! Did they get to Dr. Kenneth as well? Can they be fixed? Is there an antidote for that kind of poison?*

Is Mother all right back at home without us?

Will we ever see her again?

And there it was. That prickly feeling in Charlie's eyes again. But he remained strong and waited for the silence in the room to give way to muffled snores before allowing himself to cry. Only he hadn't even the chance to do that before a skinny, cold hand clamped over his mouth.

"Don't shout!" someone whispered, and there was Georgie, clinging to the bed railing like a very determined monkey. Charlie nodded, and Georgie slowly removed her hand.

"I don't remember you," she whispered, "but I'll admit you seem familiar."

"It's because I'm your—"

"Shush!" Georgie silenced him. "You said you came to help me. I can't explain how, but I feel like I can trust you. So, let's go. I'm ready."

"We can't just *walk* out!" said Charlie. "I need time to prepare!"

Georgie frowned. "Then you can't help me, and I'll have to do it on my own."

She began to climb back down the bedposts, and Charlie realized he'd made a mistake. Yes, he knew exactly what Georgie intended to do. If he didn't come along, she'd go it alone, and just like always, he'd be forced to keep her out of trouble. In a way, he was grateful. It meant the grandmothers didn't erase everything.

"N-no! Wait!" he whispered. Georgie paused on the floor below, looking up at her brother with skepticism.

"I can't stay here anymore," she said.

Charlie made his way down the bunk ladder like most sane people would. "I'll help you," he said, "but we have to stick together!"

"Good. Then let's go," said Georgie, and she shook Charlie's hand like they'd just made a business deal. "My name is Pigeon, by the way."

No it isn't, thought Charlie, but he didn't have time to give his sister any history lessons. He had to figure out—and fast—how they were going to make their escape. All this time, Charlie had been absorbed in the process of locating his sister. Now that he'd caught up with her again, he realized he hadn't put much thought into getting out of the cave.

Charlie looked all around the sleeping hall, beyond the thousands of beds stacked up into towers, in search of the best way out.

"We'll go that way," he said with an air of confidence he didn't actually possess.

"Are you sure?" asked Georgie.

"It's a way out of this room, isn't it?" reasoned Charlie. "That's what escape is. You get out of one room and then the next and then the next until you're free. We'll worry about the rest of the doors as we come to them."

Such reckless thinking went against every fiber of Charlie's being, but he knew that if he went *with* the grain of his being, they'd never get beyond a few feet in front of them. Naturally, the moment he thought this up, doubt seized him again, and he couldn't move an inch.

"How about this?" said Georgie reassuringly. "Let's go where you say. If we get caught, you can pretend I was sleepwalking and that you were trying to stop me. It's probably happened before anyway."

Charlie nodded nervously and, with only slight hesitation, led the way. Georgie followed, and the two children crept from the cavern with remarkably little trouble. Once Charlie thought he heard something shuffle behind them, but he didn't see anything when he looked.

"What's wrong?" asked Georgie.

"I thought I heard something," said Charlie, pausing, and then, "but maybe not."

He could not, however, rid himself of the distressing feeling that they were being followed.

"Come on!" whispered Georgie. "I think I recognize this corridor. They change all the time, you see, but some of them keep certain characteristics. Look here. This one has hatch marks on the wall, like somebody was counting days. If we go down to the end and turn left, I'm almost sure that will get us to the great hall."

But the only available corner they turned led them down a short hall that ended in a wall. Adjacent to that was a formidable metal door that turned out to be locked.

"Oh," said Georgie, disappointed.

"Hold on. I know this is going to sound strange, but maybe I can open it," said Charlie. He stared at the door handle as hard as he could. *Open up!* he thought. *Come on, door! It's important!* But unlike the last time he encountered a locked door, all he succeeded in doing now was giving himself a headache.

"What was that supposed to do?" asked Georgie, one eyebrow raised.

But in the distance, the children heard the sound of something moving toward them, and that distance was quickly getting shorter.

"Sandies!" Georgie warned.

"What?" whispered Charlie. The rag-and-bone woman had said something about "sandies," too. This was the second time the old woman's words had borne some connection to the caves.

"The sandmen?" Georgie said, but upon seeing that Charlie still didn't understand, she rolled her eyes and clarified, "The *guards*."

"Oh," said Charlie. "Why are they called sandmen?"

"Because they have magic sand that makes you forget things," answered Georgie. "Now hush!"

The noise was drawing closer, and the closer it came, the more it sounded like a breeze rustling dry tree leaves—not the marching feet of the catlike guards. And Charlie had heard this breeze before.

"I don't think those are sandies," he said.

Georgie, too, listened, and then the blood drained from her face. She began to tremble. "I didn't think they would come tonight!" she whispered.

Charlie quickly turned back to the door and grabbed its handle, squeezing as hard as he could.

"Come on, come on!" he whispered. Flashes of the bedbugs' last visit raced before his eyes while Horseshoe's tale of her poor friend's conversion into a spy repeated itself in his head. If Charlie and Georgie weren't able to get out of there very soon, he was sure they would be the bugs' next victims. And the bugs were so close. So very, very close.

"*Open! Now!*" Charlie commanded the door, and then that strange hot force, the one he had felt the terrifying night he escaped his room in the farmhouse, burst from his chest and down through his arm once more. Then the handle crumbled into pieces in Charlie's hand, and the door swung open with only a mild complaint.

Charlie grabbed Georgie's hand and pulled her with him through the doorway, closing the door again just in time for the bedbugs to make a turn down the hall. The two waited silently, holding their breath, the seconds feeling like hours. A crack under the door let Charlie glimpse the scores of beetles rushing past in an obsidian wave, and he could hear their tiny voices chanting. *Find them, find them, FIND THE LOST CHILDREN! Sad! So sad are little kiddies who run away from home!*

And then they were gone. Relief washed over Charlie like his own nervous sweat. He figured the bedbugs had probably crawled through cracks in the walls the way they fit themselves into children's ears. It didn't really matter to him how they went away, though, so long as they didn't come through that door.

There was a stench in this new chamber that brought tears to Charlie's eyes. In the dim light of a few weak torches on the walls, Charlie saw they were in an interminably long, tall room piled high with debris: crushed soup vats, broken spoons, snapped hammers. He saw heaps of ruined fabric, too, and loads of spoiled meat, the source of which Charlie didn't want to think about.

"Is this what they call the 'garden of refuse'?" he asked as he wandered through the rubbish. *I'm probably crawling with germs right now,* he thought, but germs seemed such a little thing compared to the danger they faced every moment.

Georgie wasn't saying anything. When Charlie looked back, he found her hiding behind a pile. Her eyes were as wide as dinner plates.

"You're one of them, aren't you?" she asked fearfully. "Only a grandmother could have done that with the door."

Charlie flushed with embarrassment when he thought of how his trick must have seemed. "No, no, no! I'm not one of them at all! I swear!" he insisted. "Look, would I have tried to get us both *away* from the bedbugs if I were a grandmother?"

Georgie gave her brother a wary look and wouldn't budge. "Then how are you doing it?" she asked. "Why can't I do it, too?"

"I don't know how I'm doing it," Charlie admitted. "Sometimes I just wish really, really hard for something to be, and it is. But not always. I don't know why."

Georgie started to say something, but all of a sudden, the door to the garden creaked open and someone tiptoed inside only to stumble over a lump of garbage with a horrendous crash. And who should pick himself up from the mess then but Badger Brush? The other boy briefly froze before he took off running back the way he'd come.

"Oh no," Charlie groaned. "We *were* followed!"

In answer to the commotion, another door opened elsewhere in the garden, and two sandmen stormed inside, growling and pointing directly at Charlie and Georgie. There was no time to run. They were caught without any hope of escape. Badger Brush had gotten out of there in the nick of time, but Charlie would have to act quickly to avoid the worst.

"Look, mister guards, sirs, this girl here—she sleepwalks," Charlie said, "and—and—and I was trying to keep her out of trouble!"

Georgie immediately affected a zombie-like manner, holding her arms out in front of her and moaning. The guards looked at each other and then at the children.

Charlie continued. "You see, if she gets in trouble again, Grandmother Ruby said we'll all be punished!" he lied. "Also, I th-think

the door we came through is broken. You really should have some-one look at it."

One of the sandmen grunted and pointed in the direction of the very door that Charlie had broken with his power. Then the children were pushed through it and back to the sleeping hall as if this whole incident had been nothing but a minor inconvenience to the watchmen. Charlie never thought he'd be so happy to see the towers of bunks again. He was disappointed at having failed escape, yes, but he knew that what had just happened could have been ever so much worse.

"Are you all right, Georgie?" he asked his sister. Immediately, he felt as if a cold knife had gone through his belly. Georgie stared at him in confusion. The sandmen growled to one another. *What have I done?* thought Charlie with terrible dread.

What he had done was call Georgie by her real name. A name he was supposed to have forgotten.

And yet, apart from the sandmen's initial alarm, Charlie's faux pas seemed to have gone unnoticed. Both of them were allowed to return to their own beds as if his mistake simply hadn't happened at all. For a while, Charlie really believed he'd been lucky. He thought that he would try to escape with his sister again tomorrow, that he would have a better plan by then.

But tomorrow came, and with it grave misfortune, for Georgie never turned up in the hammering hall. She was nowhere to be found.

CHAPTER EIGHT

THE QUEEN

The hammering hall began to spin as Charlie's stomach somersaulted inside him. Every crunch of clock material was a muffled roar behind the sounds of his own panicked breathing. *They took her,* he thought. *I only just found her, and now they've taken her!*

"Milkweed! Have you seen the new girl? Pigeon?" he asked the tall boy, but Milkweed refused to acknowledge Charlie—at least by words. Milkweed's wide eyes and visible gulp told Charlie enough, though. Something had happened, and the tall boy knew. Worse still, a quick glance about the hall told Charlie that *everyone* knew. It was the way they all looked at him and then darted their eyes away quickly. They knew, all right, and they were afraid.

This dark situation would only get worse, for two sandmen threw open the doors to the hall then and stormed toward Charlie with malevolent purpose in their step. Their eerie blue eyes were locked on him, unwavering. They didn't even wince at the shards of glass and metal that flew through the air all around them. *Cowards*, Charlie thought of his fellow workers as they pretended not to see the scene unfolding, *but then maybe I would do the same*.

The sandmen seized Charlie and shackled his wrists and ankles before removing him from the hammering hall with force that was hardly necessary. After all, it wasn't as if their prisoner would put up a fight.

At least, not yet.

"What's happening? Where are you taking me?" Charlie asked the sandmen, even though he knew they wouldn't answer.

The sandmen took Charlie down corridors he'd never seen before, though he wasn't sure what set them apart. In truth, these tunnels looked like every other Charlie had seen, but they *felt* strange. They felt bad.

"Are you taking me to the figment chamber?" Charlie asked. In answer, one of the sandmen bared his teeth and hissed, and Charlie kept quiet after that.

Little by little, the minimal light within these weirdly wrong corridors lessened. The floors and walls became smoother, their rocky ridges flattening along the way until everything was polished black granite. The once plain, rocky surfaces now reminded Charlie of a mausoleum, but here there were no praying cherubs, no lily garlands. Here there were only grotesque, sculpted faces staring blindly from panels on the walls. Devils and monsters and goblin heads supported torches in the most uncomfortable ways—up their noses, in their ears, buried in eye sockets. Yet for all the blazing torches these tortured sculptures held, their light had limited power over the darkness here.

At last, the sandmen and Charlie came to two great doors as black and smooth as the gem from Grandmother Opal's ring. Once they were opened, a blinding light beamed out from within. The sandmen gave their charge a shove into this new chamber and left him there, closing the doors behind him, but as soon as Charlie's eyes were able to adjust, his jaw dropped. There was no darkness in this place. Everything save the checkered floor, which seemed to go on forever, was as white as pearls. Scattered about the room were great big white statues of men and women, fashioned in the style of cemetery sculptures except that their limbs, as it happened, were twisted all wrong.

In the middle of this strange room was a gargantuan white throne, and seated there was another figure of white, though this one wore clothes. Real clothes, Charlie noted with curiosity, of black velvet and silk with beads of black pearl draped about its neck. The statue also wore a black headdress that, along with the style of its dress, made the figure look like Anne Boleyn from drawings Charlie had seen in books, except the artist here hadn't bothered to sculpt any hair onto its head. But the truly bizarre thing about this statue was that it had no eyes. Where its eyes ought to have been there was only smooth white face. Somebody had gone to the trouble of painting its lips black, though, and its mouth was a bit too wide. With the paint, it made the sculpture look like a harlequin.

Then Charlie noticed something else. Bolted in the center of the figure's chest was a filigree brooch, and in the middle of the brooch

was a keyhole. It all seemed startlingly familiar to Charlie. *But where would I have seen anything like it before?* he thought. His thoughts were soon directed elsewhere, however, for standing at either side of the throne were two characters Charlie had wished he'd never see again: the ill-tempered kitchen boy, Chicken Liver, and the hideous Grandmother Opal. Grandmother Opal stood there with a smirk on her nasty face, but Chicken Liver—he couldn't look at Charlie at all. The kitchen boy kept his eyes guiltily on his toes.

"Do you know where you are, Charlie?" asked Grandmother Opal.

"My name is Mousetrap—" Charlie began, but Grandmother Opal snarled.

"No more of these games, Charlie!" she said. "We know what's been going on. You never forgot a thing, did you? Again, *Charlie*, do you know where you are?"

"No. No, I don't," Charlie said.

This answer gave Grandmother Opal great pleasure. Chicken Liver tried to smile, but it was a weak attempt, tempered by obvious shame.

"Kneel before the Queen!" Grandmother Opal bellowed, and Charlie did as he was told, though he was thoroughly baffled over why anyone would kneel before a statue. That is, until the statue in the throne turned its head to face Charlie before rising to its feet as naturally as any living woman. This was not a *statue* of a queen. This *was* the Queen. Charlie's mouth felt very dry now, and he became aware that he hadn't closed it in quite some time.

"Rememberer," said the Queen. When she spoke, the voice of

thunder echoed across the entire chamber. Charlie felt a tremor race through his whole body.

The Queen stepped down from her throne then, her stiff black gown trailing behind her, feet making no sound. Charlie instantly cringed, but the Queen came no closer before she turned her back to him. This was how Charlie came to see her eyes glaring at him through a sheer veil of black lace. Indeed, she *did* have eyes. Three pairs of them, in fact, decreasing in size from the top pair to the bottom and trailing down the back of her head. The eyes had scarlet irises without any pupils that Charlie could see, and they never blinked. Not once. Badger Brush had been frightened by the sight of the strange queen, but for once, Charlie found himself feeling more confused than anything.

Is she really looking at me now, or is she looking at them? Charlie wondered. Face pointing one way, eyes another. Who could be sure what was what?

"Rise, Rememberer," said the Queen, "and face your foes."

It took Charlie a second to realize that she was, in fact, speaking to him. Then he awkwardly stood, his chains clanking as he did.

"It was this one who first informed us of you," said the Queen in her stormy voice, pointing a delicate finger at Chicken Liver. "He spoke of a boy who remembered, a boy who sought someone he'd lost. This one then, in the hope of reward, told my general of his suspicions."

Here, the Queen pointed languidly at Grandmother Opal. "Most High General Grandmother Opal has always been eager for advancement. She hoped to serve at my right hand as Judge. Thus, she was anxious to alert me to her findings. What a fortuitous occasion for all that you have now been found."

Charlie's blood boiled with rage. "You traitor!" he shouted at the cowed Chicken Liver. Grandmother Opal cackled. The Queen, however, merely turned around as if mildly surprised by Charlie's outburst, though her face was empty of emotion. Charlie wondered if any emotion could be revealed by a face with no eyes.

"I—I—I had to!" Chicken Liver insisted. "We were finally doing all right, you know. We hadn't had any trouble in weeks! Then *you* came along and nearly ruined everything for all of us! I did it for everyone!"

The Queen ignored her general and the tattling kitchen boy as she held out her hands. From her palms a black fluid bubbled. No. No, it wasn't fluid, Charlie soon saw, but a stream of little black bedbugs, shimmering in the white light of the room. These flowed from within the Queen's own hands and spilled between her slender fingers onto the floor.

Grandmother Opal's hands with their tarantula fingers flew to her mouth as she moaned. "No! My Queen! I beg you!" she howled, falling to her knees. "I have only ever been loyal to you!"

"What's going on? What is this?" Chicken Liver whimpered.

"Your rewards," the Queen calmly replied. The stream of bedbugs grew from a trickle to a flood, and the twin floods swarmed away from the Queen to both the cowering Grandmother Opal and the paralyzed Chicken Liver, enveloping them completely. Grandmother Opal was devoured at once, never to harm another child again. But the poor kitchen boy was carried away shrieking. All of

Charlie's hatred for the traitor evaporated at once. Whatever lay in store for Chicken Liver was bound to be worse than anything he deserved. After all, the boy had only been frightened.

"What's going to happen to him?" Charlie croaked.

"He will be fed to the phantoms."

The Queen's voice echoed for ages. To her answer, Charlie could say nothing. He wasn't sure if he could ever say anything about anything again, really. For the moment, he was entirely out of words.

"They were treacherous," the Queen explained. "They were only out to serve themselves, and they would have done you harm if given the opportunity. I would not have you harmed, Charlie Oughtt. You have a great purpose."

The Queen moved about the great throne room, slowly and *backward*. Charlie presumed this was in order to see where she walked, but it looked all manner of weird and wrong. What he would have given to run away! But his legs felt as heavy as two stone pillars, and he didn't know where he'd go if he could.

"I am most impressed by you," said the Queen, her unsettling red eyes regarding him with curiosity as she passed. "Your possession of memory is a simple matter. You sleep too little, and your mind is an impermeable fortress. What troubles your soul must bear! Alas, it is in sleep that my sandmen sow the seeds of forgetfulness, and children who remember their lives before coming to me, I regret to say, are useless here."

Charlie held his breath, waiting to hear the worst.

"You, however. You demonstrate unseen skill," said the Queen, which was not what Charlie had expected her to say. She went on.

"We have had rememberers before. We have even had rememberers who, like you, managed to pass through judgment uncaught, but they have never lasted this long."

"Never lasted this long before what?" Charlie blurted. He wished he hadn't.

The Queen stopped at once, turning her eyeless face to him. For a second, there was a flicker of a smile upon her harlequin lips. But she didn't answer his question.

"I speak of your figment, the *dream stuff in your head*," she said, quoting Badger Brush. "It is the most powerful I have encountered. Such horrors you imagine . . . such dangerous possibility you see in every detail! You could be an artist, Charlie Oughtt, and you may be of use to me yet. Of course, you will be rewarded for your service when the world is mine. Tell me. What do you remember of your life above?"

This made Charlie furious. His whole world had been turned upside down, and now this marble witch woman assumed he would serve her in exchange for whatever reward she deemed worthy. Why, she was no queen at all. She was a beast at best! A mixed-up, twisted puzzle box of a beast! And that, as far as Charlie was concerned, was that.

"I'm not going to answer any questions of yours until you answer mine," said Charlie as defiantly as he could, though his cracking voice betrayed his nervousness.

The Queen waved a hand, giving him leave to ask whatever he wished. It took him time to find his voice again. He wanted to know where his sister was, but he hoped the Queen didn't know about

Georgie. If she did, she might use her against him, or hurt her to force Charlie into service.

"Who are you people," he finally asked, "and what *is* this place? Why are you taking children?"

Charlie's heart was pounding so hard it was likely to burst out of his chest. When the Queen didn't answer at first, he was sure he had a fistful of bedbugs waiting for him, but then the Queen smiled as if she were in on a very clever secret.

"But you know me well, Charlie Oughtt," she said. "You have known me all your life. As does your mother. And her parents before her. Queen Nefertiti. Attila the Hun. Your father. From the weakest of you to the greatest, all of you have known me. And now that we are face to face, you don't recognize me. What a convenient blindness."

Charlie squinted one eye. "I'm not following," he said.

The Queen drew her breath and then blew across her palm. Instantly, a chill struck Charlie through his chest, and he shuddered. *I am so very fragile*, he caught himself thinking. *I could be crushed like an ant at any second!* His stomach churned with sudden panic, and he sank to the floor, his knees having buckled from the weight of a new and devastating fear. Fear of what in particular he couldn't rightly say. Of *everything*. This sensation was fright from concentrate. A thick, sticky syrup of despair gulped down all at once.

But then, as quickly as it had occurred, the feeling dissipated, leaving only an aftertaste of unease.

"What was that?" he rasped as he struggled to stand.

"That was my name," answered the Queen as simply as if she'd said "Jenny."

She glided back to her throne and sat, basking in Charlie's horror.

"Fear," he whispered, and for a moment he believed it. He had *felt* it. But once he'd said it aloud, he realized it made absolutely no sense whatsoever. "You're telling me you're *fear?*"

"I am terror," replied the Queen in her thunderstorm voice. "I am dread. I am the unknown within the shadows, the filament that binds the nightmares of man. But I cannot remain in the minds of men, child. I must have more."

"M-more?!" Charlie spluttered. "I mean, if you're really fear itself, haven't you already got more power than you need?"

The Queen shook her head. "Even my power has limitations," she confessed. "It is the world outside of your thoughts that I desire. The real world. But the world as you know it is not suitable for me. There is darkness in it, but not enough. There is horror, but it is too limited. And of course, I require figment. Without it, I am as much a slave to this environment as you. Tell me, dear boy, would you not change the world if you could? Do you not wish for freedom?"

Of course Charlie would change the world. He'd make it into a place without any diseases or accidents or any way for anyone to be hurt. He'd make it a place where nothing was dangerous whatsoever. But such a place would be tremendously boring to people like his sister. Even he had to admit that it was no way to live.

"How are you planning to change the world?" he asked. "There's an awful lot of it, you know."

The Queen laughed softly. It was an arrogant laugh, full of pride and amusement at Charlie's disgust. "With my harvest trees, of course," she said with a flourish of her hand. "It has taken a thousand years to create a tree that would live, but now they are scattered throughout this globe. More are being planted all the time. And my, how my deep-rooted children grow! How they thrive!"

Charlie thought of the old tree at the farm. It had been a harvest tree, he was sure of it, but it had looked as dead as dead could be.

As if the Queen had expected Charlie's confusion, she said, "Oh, but my trees are not *natural* like your oaks and elms that feed on sunlight and water. It is your figment that gives my trees their strength. This they take up through their roots from the minds of the children I give them, and when they have had their fill, they spread it throughout the world like the air that you breathe. Soon, the whole planet will be filled with figment, and I will be free to rule it and mold it to my desires."

"You can't!" Charlie gasped.

"But I have already begun," said the Queen. "It is happening as I speak to you now."

"But why? Why do you have to use children?" asked Charlie.

"Because your elders have allowed their figment to recede with the tide of their ebbing youth," answered the Queen with a sneer. "They are too *dull* to serve any purpose beyond delivering you to me. Only a child's figment is strong enough to accomplish what I desire, for only children still imagine with abandon. A child's thoughts are limitless. So, too, will I be. You see, it *must* be children. And through children I will live without bonds. Without the infection of those deceits that plague you even now—those lies of hope, love, and *courage*."

Charlie could not help but notice that as the Queen snarled those

149

last few words, she placed a hand over her heart, favoring the keyhole bolted there as if it gave her pain. Again he was reminded of the words of the rag-and-bone woman. *I had the key, but it ran away when I—* Oh, how did the rest of it go? It seemed important now, but his thoughts were darting about in his head so fast he couldn't hold on to any of them for very long.

"Alas, I am not without bonds just yet," the Queen continued. "Until the figment has coursed through every vein of this earth, I am but a shadow of myself. I do not have the strength to create my world alone. I need an architect to design it—to help me build it. A rememberer who knows fear so intimately that his nightmares are masterpieces of terror. I believe that rememberer is you."

"What makes you think I can do anything for you? I'm not special," said Charlie.

"Do you not know?" asked the Queen. "There is figment all around you here, and it is waiting for a voice to command it. Because you have your memories, you are that voice. You can move things with only your will. You can bend their form into any shape you wish simply by thinking of it."

"I . . . I can?" said Charlie. True, he *had* managed to unlock a couple of doors in highly unusual ways, but he hadn't believed those incidents to be anything more than a fluke. He'd begun to think that perhaps everyone could do it if they were panicked enough.

"The very rocks will obey your order," said the Queen. "But not every rememberer has the ability to envision such frightful things as you. It is precisely that combination of vicious imagination and command over the figment that makes you particularly valuable.

You and I are of one mind, I think, though you have not yet learned to love your fear. But you will in time."

Charlie felt his face grow hot. He didn't know what sort of person this monster thought he was, but she had another think coming if she thought he was going to help her turn his world into a living nightmare.

"What if I refuse? What if I use these so-called talents of mine to overthrow you?" he asked through clenched teeth, but the Queen only laughed.

"Overthrow me? How? By opening locked doors?" she cackled, rising from her throne. "As if you would even dare. Your little sister is far braver than you, *Charlie-O*, and your little sister is terrified."

Now Charlie was really afraid. "What do you mean? What have you done with her?" he asked, and the Queen was only too happy to tell him.

"Even now, she sits with hundreds of others in my figment chamber, the fields of dreams and wishes reaped from her little head by my harvest trees," she replied coldly. "When all her figment is used up, she will become another of my servants. She'll serve me well, I think, as a grandmother to lure in more children. My current generation has failed me in so many ways, but each generation is better than the last. All the children I harvest, whoever they were before, become my grandmothers in the end."

"You witch! You horrible, evil old witch!" Charlie exclaimed.

"You could learn to see the beauty in horror, Charlie," said the Queen, moving toward him. "The frightened cries of all the earth's creatures would be music to your ears just as they are for me. Let me teach you. Surrender your memories, and I will replace them with better ones. You need only be willing, and you could have whatever you wished."

"All I wish for is my family back!" Charlie argued.

"You could forget them and create a new family," offered the Queen, creeping ever closer, "and they would never displease you."

"Keep away from me!" Charlie shouted. He tried to run, but his legs were like stone again. The Queen reached for him as quick as a viper, grabbed the chains that bound his wrists, and pulled him close to her cruel face. Then she twisted her head around in a most frightening way, her six eyes glaring holes into Charlie's two.

"Demonstrate for me now," ordered the Queen. "Let me witness the extent of your skill."

Charlie jerked and struggled, but it was no use. The Queen had an impossible grip. Charlie wished with all his might that the irons tethering his limbs together would unlock themselves the way some doors had lately, but it was not so simple a matter when one's arms and legs were involved. Suppose he managed to mangle his hands in the process? What if he twisted his feet the wrong way around? Oh, but the Queen's red stare was too horrible to bear much longer. Worse still was the thought of Georgie becoming a grandmother like Opal. *Open up, you manacles!* he thought. *If I truly have any power at all, open up for me now!*

But other thoughts were getting in the way. What in the world was figment? What was this dream stuff that everyone kept going on about? Too many questions remained, but now was the worst time of all to be asking anything. *Focus, Charlie, focus!* he thought. *Focus on unlocking these chains!*

And then, miracle of miracles and quick as you please, both sets of irons began to rattle and click. In a split second they were open, and they clattered, chains and all, to the floor in a rusty heap. Wasting no time, Charlie turned heel and fled as fast as he could. *Open up! Open now!* he screamed inside his head at the giant obsidian doors, but he didn't have time to concentrate on the matter, and the huge slabs remained in place. So Charlie did the only natural thing and slammed his body into them with such force they had no choice but to part for him. His shoulder ached tremendously now, but he dared not stop. Nor did he ever look back, for he could hear the Queen's mad cackle of delight following him all the way.

"It is true!" she was singing. "My architect has come!"

Charlie ran down tunnels and across chambers and anywhere he could squeeze through. Meanwhile, sandmen and grandmothers alike kept fast on his heels. Other children screamed and dove for cover as he passed, but Charlie paid them no mind. All he could think about was getting away. But then the air all around him became molasses-thick, and any movement whatsoever required significant effort. *This is the Queen's doing,* he thought. Charlie fought like a champion, though, until somewhere in a dark corridor, he stumbled and fell, unable to get up again. No matter how hard he shut his eyes and concentrated, he couldn't move his own legs.

Two grandmothers quickly seized Charlie by the arms. He was afraid to guess what they would do with him now. But just as he was thinking it was curtains for him, he saw the smallest twinkle of light as something dark dashed across the path ahead. It paused, this black thing, just long enough for Charlie to make out its pointy ears and the blur of a sparkle at its throat. *Mister Gordon!* Charlie thought. He had been *sure* he'd never see the black cat again. Whether it was here to help or cause him trouble, however, there was no way he could know. He was powerless to reach the creature now, and after one of the grandmothers hissed at it, it ran off yet again. *What good are you?* Charlie thought bitterly. *You're no braver than I am.*

The air turned colder than it already was as a shadow stretched across the floor. The two grandmothers turned around at once and bowed their heads, never loosening their hold on their prisoner. Charlie craned his neck upward to see the smooth white countenance of the Queen.

"What shall we do with him, Your Highness?" asked one of the grandmothers with a greedy grin.

"Shall we feed him to the phantoms?" asked the other with a gluttonous giggle.

"Oh, please!" the two begged together. "Let us feed him to the phantoms!"

"No," said the Queen, to the visible disappointment of her ugly servants. "Not this one. He is to be taken to the Lonely Hollow, where he will sit alone in the dark without hope of escape until he chooses to serve me. And he will serve me or die, forgotten by all."

"I'll never serve you!" Charlie shouted.

"I will give you time to rethink your decision, but not long," said the Queen. "If you accept my command before it is too late, you will be saved. Delay, however, and no one will come for you. You will grow old in the darkness. Your figment—and eventually your life—

will fade with the years. What a pity it would be to see you waste away into oblivion. You who would have been my brightest light."

Charlie struggled in the iron grip of the grandmothers, but it did him no good. The grandmothers once more bowed their heads to their mistress and then dragged Charlie away until the aching cold warmed to a more bearable chill and the Queen was far behind them.

Maybe I should pretend to serve her, he thought as his boots scraped along the gritty floors. *I could pretend long enough to get her to trust me, and then . . . then maybe I could betray her and save everyone!*

But perhaps that was what she wanted, he considered. Perhaps there wouldn't be a chance for him to trick her. What if *through* him the Queen managed to do even worse things, and he was unable to stop her?

"Oh dear," he said aloud without meaning to. Whatever was he to do?

"Oh dear is right, rodent!" snapped one of the grandmothers. She had a bullish head with heavy pearl earrings that stretched her earlobes down to her shoulders. To think that she had once been an innocent child was sickening.

"It's off to the Lonely Hollow with you!" said the other through a mouth like a toad's. "Do you know what awaits you in the Hollow?"

Charlie shook his head.

"Nothing!" she answered with a snicker. "Nothingness in its purest form!"

"Empty, cold, lonely *nothing.* You'll count yourself lucky if you catch a rat nibblin' on your toeses," said the bullish one.

Charlie sighed sadly and watched the floor slide away beneath

156

him as the two grandmothers chattered between themselves. At least, he consoled himself, he wasn't being fed to the phantoms. That meant he had time to come up with a plan.

"It is a bit boring, though," said the toad mouth.

"It is, isn't it? You don't get to hear many screams from in there," said the bull head. "Just crying, and crying is so *dull.*"

"Not like with the phantoms!"

"All the other rememberers get sent to the phantoms. I can't think of why this skinny mouse would be any different."

"Neither can I! Why *should* he be different? I say."

The grandmothers stopped, still gripping Charlie by the arms.

"Careful now, Grandmother Beryl," said the bull. "I can tell what you're thinking, and we both know what *she* would do to us if we dared."

"But how would she find out, Grandmother Coral?" said the toad. "If she ever asks, we'll just say he got too old!"

"Yes, they *do* grow up quickly. . . ."

"Come, come, Grandmother Coral. Let's have us a bit of fun!"

"To the phantoms!" both grandmothers cheered, and Charlie's panic was quite renewed.

Think, Charlie, think! he commanded himself, but his imagination did not magically save him now. No one rescued him at the last split second. When the grandmothers finally stopped before a dead end, the floor simply dropped open beneath him, and then he fell in darkness forever.

CHAPTER NINE

THE PHANTOMS

At least, it seemed like forever. For ages Charlie fell. And fell. And fell. The fall took such a long time that Charlie had a moment to think over the Queen's words while he dropped. "Your little sister is far braver than you," she had said, "and your little sister is terrified." *Georgie! What have they done to you? Now I'm going to fall to my death. Or if not my death, I'll at least be shattered to smithereens and in no shape to rescue anybody.*

But Charlie was neither sent to his grave nor shattered to smithereens. When he did land, it was suddenly but gently upon wet and grassy ground. Charlie stood unsteadily and peered into the darkness. At first, that darkness was all he saw, but as his eyes adjusted, another world came into view. Yes, an entire other world with a skyline of its own! How it fit within this cavern, Charlie didn't know, but he was learning that the caves did not adhere to the same natural laws as the world above.

This new, strange world took on the appearance of a vast but un-usual city. Distant structures of all sizes lined the horizon. Some of these scraped the sky and others were very short. They all leaned in precarious directions, and their roofs jutted at angles Charlie had never seen in architecture before. Stranger yet, Charlie could see right through them as if they were ghosts. Their walls were but a green haze, their features merely an emerald halo.

This odd city possessed what appeared to be a park, and that was where Charlie stood now. Here a bench as hazy as the far-off build-ings had been set adrift in the air like a lost balloon. There were ghostly trees, too. They were all dripping something, he saw, and when the tree drops hit the ground, they turned into fallen leaves. Charlie tried to pick one up and examine it, but the glowing grass clung dearly to his boots whenever he moved.

"Yech!" Charlie said as he lifted a foot.

"*Yechhhhhh . . . ,*" came a whispering echo. Charlie looked up and jumped, his heart in his throat. Above him, swirling in the green sky like a cyclone, were even more ghostly things. Ghosts of everything. People, animals, objects—all with distorted features. Some of the people hadn't any faces at all and some only half a head.

"You're the phantoms, aren't you?" Charlie asked.

"*You are in the prison of the forgotten,*" they said with thousands of different voices all at once.

"The forgotten what? And who's forgotten them?" said Charlie.

"*We are the dreams the sleepers forget,*" the phantoms answered. "*Dreams once lived so vividly in slumber only to evaporate like dew in the sun.*"

"Oh," said Charlie. He wasn't sure what else to say, really. So he asked, "Have you always been here?"

"No," said the phantoms. "We were stolen by the Queen, and we cannot return to our home without her. Nor can she destroy us. So we are kept prisoner here, left to starve until she sees fit to feed us."

Charlie gulped. "Are . . . are you going to eat me now?" he asked, afraid of the answer.

"No," said the phantoms, and Charlie breathed a sigh of relief. But of course the ghosts *would* continue.

"Not just yet," they said, "for we have already dined quite recently. A boy not unlike you, in fact. But we will hunger again very soon, and then we will have to eat you."

"Oh," said Charlie, frowning.

"We wish that it were not so," the phantoms said sadly. "It is only your thoughts that we hunger for, but we cannot reach them from here without eating up the rest of you as well. So it must be for as long as we are captives here."

The phantoms sounded so miserable that Charlie couldn't help but pity them, even if they were intending to make a meal out of him. Not that he took the inevitable return of their appetites lightly. In fact, it was his plan to keep them talking until he could find a way out of this fix. But he felt sorry for the phantoms all the same.

"Why did the Queen steal you?" he asked them.

"Why?" hissed the phantoms. "WHY?"

Suddenly, the phantom dreams glowed scarlet and swarmed around him, making him very, very tense. "Because she is a thief and a viper!" seethed the hurricane of ghosts. "A blight! A stain upon all that is good!"

"Ohhh boy," Charlie said to himself. *Just when I was doing so well,* he thought.

"Do you know what she is, she who would have us call her 'Queen'?" they fumed.

"She told me she was fear," said Charlie, "but you're . . . you're going to tell me that's wrong, aren't you?"

The phantoms issued a noise that resembled laughter, only it was dry and distorted and alien in sound. *"She lies!"* they said, and they circled around Charlie again. *I wish they'd stop doing that,* he thought.

"She was made by fear, but she is not fear itself!" they said. *"Just as we are dreams but not the dreamers. Fear itself! That she could* think *herself so powerful!"*

"I'm afraid I don't understand," said Charlie, "but p-please don't take offense. I don't understand a lot of things down here. The Queen. The grandmothers. This figment business. None of it makes any sense at all to me. Though if you all say you're forgotten dreams, I'm not going to doubt you."

"Bah!" spat the phantoms. They slowed their furious swirling, and their color cooled to a greener hue. It seemed to Charlie that they had all become quite depressed again.

"Forgive us. Of course you don't understand," they said, their myriad voices drenched with woe. *"You should not be here, child. None of you should. Nor should we."*

Charlie thought they were all as mad as hatters, but he dared not say so as long as they were calm again.

Then the phantoms drifted up, up into the sky, where they formed a ring. *"Look, boy, and see,"* they said. *"As long as you are waiting to die, you should know who feasts upon you."*

"Thanks," Charlie said dryly.

In the center of that ghostly ring, a most unusual picture appeared from nothing. It looked like the night sky as Charlie imagined it from far beyond the earth, black as ink and glittering with stars. And stretching throughout the inky expanse were vaporous clouds in vibrant colors. It was frightening and beautiful all at once.

"What is that?" Charlie murmured.

"*It is home,*" the phantoms answered.

"Home . . . for dreams?"

"*For dreams, yes, and for all of your thoughts, ideas, and notions.*"

"But my thoughts, ideas, and notions live in my head," said Charlie, "where they're made. Or don't they?"

Charlie suddenly had the sense that his understanding of things was about to be quite shaken up. It was an idea that would've frightened him a great deal once, but as he was due to be eaten any time now, information seemed the least of his problems.

"*Your thoughts do not stay within you once you have thought them, child,*" said the phantoms. "*Nor do they cease to exist once forgotten. Indeed, they are living beings, given their life by the magic inside your head. We call this magic your figment. It cannot be seen, cannot be touched— not by you. Yet even now it is creating empires.*"

Charlie found himself quite speechless. He thought about what he was seeing and then wondered if those very thoughts were alive just now. And then if *that* thought was alive. And *that* one, too. Then he decided to stop thinking about it at all because it would only give him a headache.

"*You little creatures are masters of a universe you can never enter,*" said the phantoms, "*another world outside all time and space that is* home to every notion you've ever had. It is where your reveries live on. Where your wishes have wishes of their own. Its very atmosphere is made of the same magic that created all the thoughts that inhabit it."

As Charlie watched, the picture above him changed, and the sights he saw were dizzying. He saw rooms that changed from royal ballrooms into dark dungeons into modern parlors not different from his own. He watched semi-transparent people walk through each other and become animals on the other side. A volcano suddenly blinked into existence and erupted scarlet ribbons while a lady in knight's armor rode by in a bathtub that walked on lion's feet.

"My thoughts end up *there?*" he asked.

"*Yours and those of others,*" said the phantoms. "*They travel there by the Unseen Road—a system of invisible paths that tie each of you to our world. There your thoughts devour one another, each becoming something new and wonderful—and terrible, too. These new creations are the dreams that return to you as you sleep, to inspire new thoughts that will continue the cycle. Only dreams are allowed to travel the Unseen Road the other way.*"

"And that's what you are," said Charlie.

"*Yes, but . . . ,*" said the phantoms, hesitating before they continued, "*not all dreams are the same. We who speak to you now were too weak to take root and grow within you, and so we were forgotten. All forgotten dreams travel home again to consume more thoughts and become even better than before. All, that is, except for us.*"

"Because you were stolen," said Charlie.

Something dark disturbed the picture then. It began as a very small blot, but it quickly grew to drape all the things Charlie saw in

shadow. These shadowy things then lost their shape and any unique characteristics they once had as they were absorbed into the spreading blackness.

"*Once in a while, a bad thing is made,*" said the phantoms. "*A thing that is not a dream, that does not wish to be part of our circle of life. Such vile creations are a plague and almost impossible to destroy. The Queen is one such . . . thing. A thing born from eons of fearful and despairing thoughts, the very worst thoughts of all.*"

A shiver raced down Charlie's spine, but he had to know more. "Go on," he said.

The phantoms continued. "*Like all bad things, she wanted power,*" they said. "*Not content to join with other notions, she desired a world of her own, and she chose yours.*"

"But only dreams can travel the Unseen Road the other way," remembered Charlie. "That's why she stole you, isn't it?"

"*Now you understand,*" said the phantoms. "*She came here on the backs of stolen dreams and has spent a thousand years harvesting your figment to prolong her life. It is also the source of her power, a power she will use to turn your world into a place of horror and eternal darkness. That is why she blots out your memories, boy. Without them, you are lost and easily harvested. Your figment is a blank canvas on which to paint her wicked purpose.*"

"But why won't she let you go?" asked Charlie. "She's got what she wants now. Why not free you?"

The phantoms issued a collective sigh. It felt cool on Charlie's face.

"*She cannot,*" they said. They abandoned the picture they had made in the sky and settled low to the ground, a mist full of misshapen faces.

"Only her destruction will send us back. We hunger always for more thoughts, but outside of our land, there are never enough for us. Thus, she keeps us trapped here in this cavern, where we cannot cause her any trouble."

"That's terrible," Charlie said softly. "I'm sorry she's done this to you."

But now the phantoms were vibrating. They had gone all red again, and they were showing their teeth. Even the trees had teeth, which was more than a little discomfiting.

"Better this than to serve her as a slave like the sandmen!" raged the phantoms. "They, too, were stolen dreams, but not weak and forgettable like we. They have no hunger. Such wonders they would have inspired had they reached their destinations! But now they are mute beasts and nothing more!"

The phantoms were drawing nearer, much too close for Charlie's comfort.

"We suffer as captives," the phantoms moaned. "The Queen gives us only a few children a week. So bitter! So foul! Imagine if you required fruit but were given the roots of its trees. But it is all we have been given, boy, and now we have been given you."

"Listen here—" said Charlie.

"We have enjoyed our palaver," said the phantoms, "but we regret it is time to conclude. Our hunger returns."

The phantoms closed in around Charlie, ghostly tongues flicking at him. *Oh, do something, Charlie! Anything!* he thought desperately, but there wasn't anything to be done. There were no chains to unlock. The only door he knew of was far above him, and he could not fly.

Then Charlie thought of something. Certainly it was true that *he* could not fly. The phantoms, however, could.

"Wait!" Charlie shouted with such volume that the forgotten dreams were momentarily stunned. He said, "What if I can get you all out of here?"

"And how would you be able to do that?" the phantoms asked.

Charlie exhaled slowly and, trembling, introduced himself properly. "My name is Charlie Oughtt," he said with a faltering voice, "and I'm a rememberer."

Those phantoms who had eyes narrowed them and glared at Charlie with suspicion. *"We've had our share of rememberers, boy,"* they said. *"If you were given to us, you cannot have made it past the grandmothers' judge. If you couldn't get that far, how are we to believe you can help us now?"*

"But I *have* made it past the judge!" said Charlie. "I've been in the caves for days. I've met the Queen *personally*. It was a mistake that got me tossed down here! Honest, it was! I was supposed to be forgotten, too."

"Why should we believe you? How do we know you're not simply trying to keep us from eating you?"

"I've already had some practice at unlocking doors and chains and things. The Queen even called me her architect!" Charlie insisted. "She said I have a gift! She offered to teach me how to use it."

All at once, the phantoms shrieked. *"Did you accept?"* they screeched. *"Did you accept her offer?"*

"No. N-no! Of course not!" Charlie answered.

This appeared to please the phantom dreams, but they weren't quite satisfied yet. "*Suppose you do let us out,*" they said. "*What then? The Queen is far more powerful than we. She would have us imprisoned again very soon. How do you propose to prevent that?*"

"I'll find some way to trap the grandmothers," Charlie offered.

"*The grandmothers!*" the phantoms laughed. "*They are hardly a threat to anyone but themselves. Even their shadow rings are mere shadows to us. And to you children, for that matter.*"

"Well, then I . . . ," Charlie began. *I don't know,* he thought. *I haven't a clue in the world.* But the phantoms were awaiting his answer, and they weren't going to settle for vague promises.

"I mean to destroy the Queen," he finally said. *I do?* he thought, unsure of what he'd just declared.

"*A heroic notion, but you cannot hope to succeed.*"

"What do you mean I can't?" said Charlie. "There must be a way!"

"*If what you say is true, you have a better chance than most,*" said the phantoms. "*You can do what other children here cannot—more than rattle chains. Given time, you could unravel the Queen's domain. But you must understand that even with all that power, you cannot hope to destroy her. The true battle is one for which no one can prepare. Do not condemn yourself to such a fate, boy. To be consumed by us would be a mercy.*"

"Tell me about this battle," Charlie said. "Please."

The phantoms all shook their heads, and for a moment, Charlie feared they would not answer him. But after a time, they spoke again.

"*There is a key,*" they said. "*The Queen knows not where it is. She cannot so much as touch it without pain, and she does not possess the* power to destroy it, for it was not she who created it. Just as fear made her, it was courage that made her weaknesses. Find this key, Charlie Oughtt. The Queen cannot be undone otherwise."

"The key . . . the two-faced queen . . . ," Charlie murmured, remembering the words of the old rag-and-bone woman again. "That's the rest of it! 'I had the key, but it ran away when I gave my names to the two-faced queen!' That's what the old woman was trying to tell me! But that would mean she *knew*. How could she have known? She's not a child, and the Queen said only children would do!"

"*Perhaps she was a child once,*" said the phantoms. "*The Queen has spies. Humans like you who can do her work where the figment has not yet spread. Children who were once rememberers but believed her promises and were betrayed. It is good that you refused her. You are a threat to her. She would offer you the world in exchange for the surrendering of your memory, but you cannot accept or you will serve her forever. Your mind will be separated from you and ground into the sandmen's dust.*"

"The old woman was trying to warn me," Charlie said sadly. "She was like me once, and she was trying to warn me! Only there wasn't enough of her left to make much sense anymore. She gave her names—her memory—to the Queen."

"*Listen!*" hissed the phantoms impatiently. "*Over the Queen's heart there is a keyhole. With the key, you must unlock her, but beware! The fear-born queen knows much, and she knows that you little creatures fear pain more than anything else in the world. She holds within herself a copy of all the most painful memories she has ever seen. And she has seen them all, child, even yours. Should you manage to unlock her, you will succeed in the destruction of her physical form, but doing so will release*" all the bad memories she keeps within her just for you. They are different for everyone, and you are not the first she has faced."

"She told me I was!" Charlie harrumphed.

"More of her lies," the phantoms continued. "If you should succumb to the pain of these memories, your pain will restore her, and when the Queen returns, she will be stronger than she was before. Then you will be her slave until another rememberer defeats her. This no one has done."

But the phantoms were wrong. Of this, Charlie was certain. He knew very well what his worst memory was. He had been reliving it ever since the night his father died. This would not be an easy fight for him, no, but he believed he was more prepared than most. Meanwhile, time was ticking away, and his sister was in mortal danger.

"If that's what I have to do, then that's what I have to do," said Charlie. "Take me up to the door. I'm ready."

"Child—"

"If I go now, I might have a chance of getting my sister out before I fight the Queen."

The phantoms sighed again. "Do you truly mean to set us free?" they asked. "Even though we tried to eat you?"

"I . . . I mean it," said Charlie. "That's a promise."

"We fear that our time of freedom will be short," said the phantoms, "but to sup upon a few grandmothers would be a fine respite, however briefly we may enjoy it. Ready yourself, Rememberer. We forgotten dreams are very cold."

The phantoms gathered around Charlie, lifting him into the air. To be held by their ghostly appendages felt like bathing in ice, but it was a whole lot better than being eaten.

When they reached the very top of the shaft, Charlie willed the trapdoor to open. It was ever so much easier to do now that he knew his power was real and understood its nature. But as soon as the door was open, he leaped through it and slammed it shut again, locking it before the phantoms could escape.

"NO!" he could hear the ghost dreams howl on the other side. "YOU MADE A PROMISE!"

"I'm sorry!" he said before he turned and fled. And as he ran, he heard the screams of the enraged phantom dreams fading with the distance.

"BETRAYER!" they screamed. "BETRAYER!"

The phantoms were unpredictable anyway, Charlie told himself. There was no way of knowing when they would lose their taste for grandmothers and go after children again. He had seen how they lost their temper so quickly. Well, he had! And he knew how suddenly their hunger could overtake them. *Anyone would do the same,* he thought.

But no amount of reason could allay his disappointment in himself for not being braver.

CHAPTER TEN

SPOONS AND HAMMERS

Charlie rushed down empty corridors, his brain humming with questions. The phantoms had said that a simple key would start the Queen's destruction. But where was this key? What did it look like? How could he even take time to look for it when Georgie's figment was being harvested that very moment? He had precious little time to figure out a rescue plan as it was. He couldn't simply walk into the figment chamber and take her. He didn't even know how to get there.

Charlie stopped, panting, and looked to his right and to his left. He had no idea where he was. Georgie could've pointed out the unique traits of any tunnel, but to him they all looked the same. *I can get myself out of chains in ways Harry Houdini only wishes he could, and yet I'm hopeless without a guide!* he thought, pulling his hair.

Just then, something furry brushed against his ankle, and he nearly yelped. But when he looked down, he saw it was only the black cat again, racing around his legs so fast that he couldn't make out its exact shape.

"Go away, Mister Gordon," Charlie said under his breath. "I don't have time for you right now. Shoo!"

But the cat refused to leave. It crossed between Charlie's legs this way and that way and back again, threatening to call attention to him should anyone pass, or to at least trip him and give him a nasty scrape on the knees. Mister Gordon demanded to be followed, it seemed, and would not allow Charlie to go anywhere that wasn't in the feline's plans.

Charlie groaned in frustration. "Stop it, you! You're only wasting my time, and I'd like to get to the figment chamber *without* manacles—*ow!*"

Mister Gordon gave Charlie a nip on the ankle before scampering down the tunnel ahead. Charlie groaned again and followed because, after all, why not? He hadn't the foggiest idea where he was going on his own anyway.

"I'm trusting you, you know! That's saying a lot!" he said.

After six turns down four corridors (two requiring a second visit), Mister Gordon finally came to a stop, the object attached to the cat's chest swinging and reflecting light from out of nowhere as usual. The light always gave Charlie a strange feeling—something like having a forgotten word on the tip of his tongue. Charlie stood there, lost in that feeling of inexplicable familiarity for a moment before he snapped out of it, looked up, and saw where they stood.

Mister Gordon had taken him to a pair of wide wooden doors,

into which were carved matching trees. *I've seen these before,* Charlie thought. Harvest trees, he figured. Yes, that was it! They were harvest trees just like the old tree on the farm!

"You did it, Mister Gordon! Thank you!" Charlie whispered, but the black cat was already gone. It hardly mattered now. Charlie had made it to the figment chamber. The question now was how to get inside. Without knowing what lay on the other side of those doors, planning for a sneaky entrance was nearly impossible whether he was some sort of figment sorcerer or not. If only, he wished, there were a way to look inside without opening the doors at all.

Charlie stared hard at the door, looking for some object he could move, some shape he could bend that would allow him to see what lay within. He stared until he'd given himself a throbbing headache, but nothing was apparent to him.

And then he felt like a fool. For right there before him was a keyhole as plain as day. Light already beamed through it like a tiny beacon. No magic was required. *Some sorcerer I am,* he thought, and he crouched before the lock to peek inside. But the sights he saw through that minuscule hole made him forget to breathe. For within lay the biggest room yet, filled with row upon row of benches. And at the benches sat numerous children—too numerous to count. All faced the front of the room, where a white sheet as tall as a house hung, and onto the sheet such awful images were projected. The images moved like pictures from a cinematograph, but they were in color and frightfully realistic.

Charlie saw tornadoes carrying off houses, teeth falling out, scenes of surprise school exams where you don't know any of the

answers. He was so horrified he had to look away at times, but all the children within the chamber sat perfectly still. That was truly the most horrible sight of all, for attached to each and every child's head was a green, glowing root. These roots came down from the high ceiling, and Charlie realized they belonged to the harvest trees aboveground.

It made Charlie's blood run cold, and he understood with an even icier chill that there were far more harvest trees than he'd ever imagined. He had seen only one at the farm, but with so many roots and so many children, there must have been hundreds! It made sense to Charlie, as much as anything could make sense in such a distorted place, that if time could be squeezed down so that it ran faster here, it was just as likely that space worked the same way. Belowground, one roomful of roots might support all the harvest trees the Queen and her servants had sown the world over. Aboveground, they may have been hundreds of miles apart.

Charlie remembered the digging he had heard one terrifying night at the farm and felt sick. The grandmothers must have been planting more. *So many!* he thought. *How can I possibly get in there through that web of roots, find Georgie, whisk her out, and all without getting both of us in a worse pickle than we're already in?*

He crept from the door and hid in a dark corner while he thought of a plan. *If only I could destroy the Queen right now. Then I wouldn't have to worry about anything else.* But to do that, Charlie needed to find the key. He wished that nuisance of a cat would appear now and lead him to the key the way it had led him to the figment chamber. He could picture the creature now. Never any clearer than a blur.

Always running away. Forever obscured by the inexplicable glare of the bauble it wore around its—

Charlie's breath caught in his throat. "Oh, I'm an *idiot!*" he said.

It had been right in front of him all along. *I had the key, but it ran away,* the old rag-and-bone woman had said. And how Grandmother Pearl had ranted at the sight of the cat nearby!

It made perfect sense. Charlie might never know where the cat had come from, but he was certain of one thing: it carried the key. And while he couldn't be sure, he had a feeling that it *wanted* to be found by him. And if it wanted him to find it, it would surely be nearby.

Charlie turned and raced through the tunnels again, stopping every time he thought he saw something move. But it was never the black cat. It was always just shadows.

"Where are youuuu?" he whispered. "Are you hiding behind the rocks?"

Get a move on, rocks! he ordered the rubble with his thoughts, and just as the Queen had told him they would, the rocks wobbled and then rolled out of the way to reveal whatever might have been behind them. Charlie was very pleased at his success, of course, but the cat was not lurking behind.

"Please, Mister Gordon! I'm running out of time!" Charlie pleaded as he turned a corner . . . and found himself directly in the path of an entire *pack* of grandmothers.

"There! A boy!" shouted one of them. The others looked all about themselves in alarm.

"Right there, you idiots!" screeched the first one, pointing at Charlie. "Right in front of you!"

"Sorry! Gotta go!" Charlie said, and he took off for the nearest turn, cursing himself for his carelessness at the same time. A few paces down, he took another turn, but it was a dead end.

"Why's a boy running out *here?*" he heard a grandmother shout.

"Where'd he run to? He can't've gone far!" said another.

Charlie hid in the darkest corner, praying that the grandmothers weren't smart enough to check for him in a blind alley. Meanwhile, their deep voices were getting louder all the time.

"Is it Mousetrap? The one *she* wanted?"

"Nah, it couldn't be! He's rotting away in the Lonely Hollow! Nobody gets out of the Hollow! Must be another brat."

Charlie felt in the darkness for something to throw. When his fingers found a pebble, he crept just to the edge of the crossing path and threw the pebble as far away from himself as he could manage, listening as it bounced with a *tick-tack-tack* off the walls down the tunnel.

"There!" barked one of the grandmothers. "Hear that? He's gone that way!"

"You four follow the sound! I'll stay right here to catch him in case he gets loose of you," said another.

Charlie crawled back and pressed himself as far into his corner as he could, cold sweat dripping down his face. *Trapped!* he thought. There were grandmothers at either end of his escape route now. The only way out was behind him, and that was just a wall. *I wish I hadn't been such a coward about the phantoms,* he thought. *They could've fixed this. Then there wouldn't be any grandmothers.*

Charlie felt behind him for something—*anything*—that he

could manipulate with his newfound powers to escape. All the time, he held his breath, as if breathing might frighten away what little good fortune remained available to him. Soon, he found a thin but distinct crack running up and down the wall. *Time to up the ante*, he thought. Squeezing his eyes shut, he pictured that sliver spreading wider and wider yet. Then, sweet merciful heavens, he heard the wall rumble. Then after that, a cool breeze ruffled the hair on the back of his head. Charlie looked around to admire the hole he had made. It was dark on the other side, but he had a better chance in there than in a dead end between grandmothers. He jumped through without another thought and then closed up the hole before he could be seen.

The room on the other side was darker than he had realized it would be. In fact, it was so dark that Charlie couldn't find his own feet. Or the wall he had just come through, for that matter. Or anything at all. There was an awfully empty feeling in the space, too. It was the kind of emptiness that went beyond bare floors and walls—the kind of emptiness one feels when one has run out of hope.

"Well, that's just great," Charlie said to himself. "I've gone and put myself in the Lonely Hollow."

Charlie walked carefully through the darkness with his arms out in front of him, feeling for any obstacles. There was nothing, good or bad, and no end to the nothingness. But just when he was beginning to think he'd well and truly gotten himself into trouble, he saw something. Despite the absence of any light in this place, what did Charlie see but a twinkle in the darkness?

"I knew you'd find me, Mister Gordon!" said Charlie, and he lurched for the spark of light to sweep the source up from the ground. It felt wet in his hands and was smaller than he'd expected. Its tail was strangely dry and scaly.

You'll count yourself lucky if you catch a rat nibblin' on your toeses, someone had said to him quite recently.

"A rat!" Charlie squeaked and, sure enough, the little light that had seemed so promising before turned out to be from a pair of glowing teeth that promptly clamped down upon the meat of his hand.

"Augh!" he cried. He dropped the creature at once, and it scurried away screeching.

This is hopeless, Charlie thought. But the very moment this thought entered his head, he felt something else there. It was as if he had forgotten a very important detail and was just beginning to re-member it again. He'd felt it before, and now he knew what it meant.

"Is it you this time?" he asked. In answer, another light twinkled, and now Charlie was certain.

"Stay where you are, Mister Gordon!" he begged. "Please don't run away again!"

This time, Mister Gordon waited. The cat waited until Charlie reached it, and when he did, it allowed Charlie to scoop it up, purr-ing as if to say, *Good job. You weren't ready before, but now you've earned it.* And then, just like that, the cat vanished. Its warm, furry body was simply no longer there. Yet the light persisted. Charlie stared in disbelief at his hands. In them rested only a shimmering golden key. It was then that he realized the cat *was* the key! Had it ever really been a cat, or had he seen only what he wanted to see? Well, it hardly mattered now. The key was his. He lifted it up high so that its light could be his guide, and it revealed a door to his left.

"You turned up right where you wanted me to be, didn't you?" he whispered to the key. He couldn't be sure, but he thought its light might have pulsed a little in reply.

Charlie pocketed the key and then tried the door. It opened easily and, trusting that the key wouldn't have led him anywhere dangerous, he stepped inside without a second thought.

Only to find himself standing in the bustling kitchen.

Fortunately for Charlie, he was obscured enough by a puff of steam from the machines that no one caught sight of him immediately. *What do I do? Oh, what do I do?* he thought, all in a panic. There were too many people here to try and slip past. After the treachery of Chicken Liver, he couldn't trust that no one else would tattle. It didn't help that Grandmother Jewel kept a very close watch on her kitchen. He might save a few seconds by pretending to be hard at work, but she would soon notice him and remember him from before.

That was when he spotted Badger Brush. The boy was carrying a giant scrubber brush. The day must nearly be over, Charlie realized. He must be on his way to clean his station. Most of the other children were still stirring stinking soup, but they, too, would be draining and cleaning very soon. Then Charlie struck upon an idea.

He waited for another cloud of steam to cover him and then scrambled to the vat Badger Brush was walking toward. Charlie climbed up the ladder and checked to make sure the vat had been emptied. Finding that it had been, he swung his legs over the side and climbed down the inner rungs to wait within. Even though the soup had been drained, the stench was just as vile as if it hadn't been, and little puddles of steaming muck remained at the bottom. Charlie's eyes watered until everything was blurry, and it was all he could do not to yell for Badger Brush to hurry.

Finally, Charlie heard the slap of bare feet climbing up outside, and it wasn't long before Badger Brush's face emerged over the rim.

"Pssst! Badger!" Charlie whispered.

"Huh? Oh!" Badger Brush gasped, and in his surprise he dropped his soapy scrubber brush, narrowly missing Charlie's head. Then he grabbed the spoon from the side of the vat and held it up defensively.

"What do you want, *ghost?*" he hissed.

"What? I'm not *a ghost!*" said Charlie. Then he remembered his bleary eyes and exceptionally disheveled appearance. "Oh gosh. No, it's not what it looks like. I'm perfectly alive! Alive and standing in the leftover soup."

"Oh, Mousetrap!" Badger Brush whispered, and he relaxed. "Golly, am I glad to see you're all right! I thought for sure I'd gotten you in trouble after that incident in the garden, and I've been expecting you to haunt me all this time!"

"Is that a thing that happens here?" asked Charlie.

"Heck if I know, but would you be surprised if it did?" said Badger Brush.

"No, not really," said Charlie, but just as he was about to explain his presence there, Badger Brush suddenly looked away.

"Hush!" he whispered. "Grandmother Jewel is coming over!"

"What are you doing up there, boy?" Charlie heard Grandmother Jewel say. "What are you standing over an empty kettle hugging a spoon for?"

"I'm airing it out, ma'am," Badger Brush lied. "They stir better with a bit of air in them."

Grandmother Jewel guffawed. "You ninny!" she said. "Get back to work! Airing out the *spoon*. Of all the ridiculous things I've ever heard!"

She moved on to scold someone else, and Badger Brush leaned over the side again. "How did you get here?" he asked.

"It's complicated," said Charlie, "but listen. There's something I need you to do."

"I suppose I do owe you one," said the other boy.

Charlie went on. "Remember what you said about creating diversions? I need you to create one now, and I need as many of you to help as possible. The thing is, I need you to stir the soup the wrong way."

Badger Brush drew his breath sharply and paled. "But that would make an awfully big mess, and the trouble we'd get into!" he said.

Charlie sighed. "I knew it was too much to ask," he said. "I suppose I'll have to ask someone else. Someone who isn't so scared of the grandmothers. Not that I *blame* you, of course . . ."

Charlie waited. He felt a bit like a bully now, but he could think of no other way than appealing to Badger Brush's pride. If this diversion worked, he'd be able to slip out of the kitchen while Grandmother Jewel dealt with the fires. It wouldn't do for him to attract any attention if he planned to go after the Queen. *Badger Brush will understand when it's all over*, he thought.

Meanwhile, the other boy flushed red. "Scared of the grandmothers! Who's scared of the grandmothers?" he said, puffing out his chest. "You just leave it to me, Mousey. We'll get some fireworks going in here like those old bats have never seen!"

"Thank you!" Charlie said. "And, Badger—"

"Yeah, what?"

"Be careful. I mean it. I wouldn't ask this of you if I could think of anything else, but it's the best I've got. There's something important I have to do. It's for all of us."

Badger Brush gulped and nodded. Then he straightened up and laughed. "Hey, I've got this under control. Don't you worry! You're the one who has to be careful, you fugitive," he said. He sprinted off, leaving Charlie alone to wonder if he'd just doomed one of the only friends he had in this place.

Charlie climbed back up the inner ladder and looked over the edge, watching as Badger Brush sneaked from one vat to another, whispering in the ears of his fellow cooks. Some of the children shook their heads, but a few looked eager to take on the challenge. Soon, they were spreading the word as well. It didn't really matter if everyone participated or not. Charlie only needed just enough of a disaster that Grandmother Jewel couldn't simply point her ring at one fire and be done with it before he had a chance to escape.

Then it began. The bubbling, the belching of the muck, the sparks and the flames. Grandmother Jewel was spitting mad, but every time she put one fire out, another started.

"I don't know what's happened, ma'am!" Badger Brush lied. "It's like something's gotten into the soup! I told you the spoons needed airing!"

Charlie almost laughed but remembered he had work to do. He

climbed down from the vat and sped through the chaos, holding his breath from the smoke until he made it to the other side of the main doors. Grandmother Jewel was so busy cursing and zapping out flames that she never saw him. *Thank you,* he thought of the kitchen children. He wished he could tell them how grateful he was, but that would have to wait. Charlie had a plan forming in his mind, and that plan now included the hammering hall.

The hammering hall would be an easier venture than the kitchen and the figment chamber. He knew the layout well, and what's more, he knew how much Grandmother Ruby adored the sound of her own voice. As long as she was talking, she wasn't likely to catch sight of walls opening up of their own accord. Nor was she likely to notice an extra head among her workers. At least, not right away.

It was a simple matter for Charlie to crawl among the piles of broken clocks until he found Milkweed. Once there, he picked up a forgotten hammer and set to smashing at clocks just to blend in.

"Milkweed," he said, perhaps too softly for the tall boy to hear him. He said again, "*Milkweed!*"

Milkweed looked around, and when he saw Charlie, he jumped a little. But then he quickly regained his composure and turned away, pretending as poorly as always that he had never seen his former workmate.

"You," said Milkweed, freeing his hammer from a gouge in the floor and hoisting it up high over his shoulder. "We thought you were a goner." *Smash!*

"I almost *was* a goner," he said, "and if anyone finds out I'm here now, I really will be. I came back because I need your help."

Crash! Crack! Bang! Milkweed didn't say anything. He just kept cracking away at his work pile. But Charlie could tell by the boy's face that he was thinking. Charlie ducked behind a pile of clocks as Grandmother Ruby made her rounds.

"Smash them! *Destr-r-r-roy* them! Strike each clock before it can strike another hour!" she shouted, pounding one fist into her palm. Her voice was like that of a parrot whose owner only ever taught it to say rude things. As soon as Grandmother Ruby was out of ear-shot, Charlie popped back up again.

"You said rememberers can do things . . . that if I figure it all out, I can maybe help you," he continued. Milkweed said nothing. "Well, I *can*. Do things, I mean. You were right."

Milkweed gave him a sideways glance and waited for further explanation. So Charlie gave him one in the form of a demonstration, pointing at an intact alarm clock and lifting it high into the air without touching it. The tall boy's eyes grew wide as he watched the clock twirl in time with the motion of Charlie's hand. Then Charlie clapped once, and the clock crashed into pieces on the ground.

Milkweed gaped wordlessly. "What kind of help do you need?" he finally muttered, and Charlie could have leaped for joy.

"Tell the others it's time," he said. "Tell them they have nothing to worry about—the grandmothers can't hurt all of you together."

Charlie hoped Milkweed would understand what he was suggesting. He knew that the boy and his fellows had something up their sleeves, and that they'd been waiting for the right person to make it possible for them to do it. Charlie didn't know what that was exactly, but he had his ideas.

"Some of them have those rings—" said Milkweed.

"Those rings can't really hurt us," said Charlie, and then he added, "Besides, *you've* got hammers. You can break through barriers and things. Who'd be able to stop you?"

"What do we do once we get out of here? We can't free everyone by ourselves," said Milkweed.

"Get to the figment chamber first and free the kids inside," said Charlie. "Their time is running out faster than anyone else's. When you're done there, take *those* kids and move on to the other chambers. I'll take care of the rest."

Milkweed paused for a long while, and Charlie was afraid he would refuse. He wouldn't have blamed Milkweed if he had. But after a while, the tall boy curtly nodded. Then he heaved his hammer over his head again and said, "You'd better go now. Grandmother Ruby's coming." *Crash!* went the hammer.

"Thank you!" said Charlie, ducking again. "Now I have to go and make good on a promise."

Charlie didn't stick around long enough to watch Milkweed's army take action, but as he fled the hall, there started a pattern of hammering he'd heard once before.

REMEMBERER! REMEMBERER! REMEMBERER!

It was time to free the phantoms. Charlie couldn't put it off any longer. He'd been a shameful coward before, but now he had to make things right. More than that, though, he thought a little guiltily, he needed them now. Charlie just hoped they could forgive him, and that they wouldn't gobble him up straightaway when they saw him.

189

"*THE BETRAYER DARES RETURN!*" they screamed when he landed on the familiar clinging grass.

"Look, I'm sorry about before," Charlie told them, and he really was, "but I've kept my promise. See? I've come back to set you free."

"*Why did you trick us?*"

"I . . . I was scared," said Charlie, "but I'm here now, and I won't trick you again. Just promise me one thing, all right? Promise you'll eat only the grandmothers. No children."

"*You will lose,*" said the phantoms.

"What?"

"*No one has ever defeated the Queen. You will lose,*" they said, "*but because you dare to try, little betrayer, we will make this promise you ask.*"

Before Charlie could say another word, the phantoms grabbed Charlie and flew him up to the trapdoor. He had scarcely opened it when they flew out the door and away, howling with delight.

"Only the grandmothers!" he called out as he ran after them. Already the bellows and shrieks of grandmothers under attack sounded in the distance. Now Charlie could only hope that, with the phantoms on the loose and the fires raging in the kitchen, any remaining grandmothers would be too preoccupied to stop Milkweed's army from reaching the figment chamber. That is, if Milkweed and his army still had their courage. *Someday,* he thought, *we'll all be able to laugh about this.* He wasn't sure how; it was just something people said when they were scared.

Charlie made a turn to take a tunnel, but the tunnel he intended was not where he found himself. Instead, he found himself standing before a familiar pair of huge obsidian doors.

"What?" he said aloud. How had he come to the Queen's throne room so fast?

Charlie looked back but found no trace of his path here. There was only the long, dark corridor he had seen once before with its polished black granite walls and tortured goblin sconces. Two of these were newer additions, he noticed, and they were faces he recognized. One had a bullish head, the other a mouth like a toad.

But there was no one alive in this hall. No one but himself. He couldn't even hear the grandmothers screaming anymore.

Charlie was utterly alone.

CHAPTER ELEVEN

THE WORST MEMORY

All right, self.

There's no getting out of it now. You're going to fight the Queen and set the world right again, and that's all there is to it. You're not going to let her scare you, either.

Because she'll try. She'll darn well try.

Speech to himself concluded, Charlie cracked his neck and then his knuckles despite his fears of arthritis. He inhaled, he exhaled, and then he shoved open the doors to the Queen's chamber with bravado he didn't really feel.

But something wasn't right. The chamber was much darker than it had been the last time Charlie stood there, when he quivered before the marble throne while beetles devoured Grandmother Opal in front of his very eyes. And those white statues, once upright and twisted in unnatural positions—they had been broken into pieces. Some of those pieces lay scattered about the checkered floor. Others hovered in the air, as if some invisible cord that once tethered them to the earth had since been snipped. *What happened here?* he thought. It looked like the Queen had thrown a most undignified temper tantrum.

As he wandered carefully through the Queen's disordered domain, Charlie was reminded of the odd prison the phantoms inhabited. It was the phantoms who had told him the Queen would use Charlie's worst memory against him. Certainly no memory could be worse than the night he lost Father. It was a memory that had haunted Charlie incessantly for all these six years. He was hardened to it, he believed. *I can't even cry when I want to,* he thought. This was a battle that tragedy had molded him to win. But where was the Queen now?

It was as if Charlie's question was the invitation, for as soon as he thought it, laughter rumbled stormily throughout the chamber. There was no mistaking whose laughter it was. Charlie froze, but not out of fear this time. No, this time it was determination that kept him firmly in place. He felt in his pocket for the key, pressing its ridges into the palm of his hand until it hurt.

A few feet before Charlie, the floor began to warp and ripple. Up from a black square welled a dark shape, a fluid column of black-and-white streaks that twisted around and around in a hypnotic spiral until the column took the form of his most dangerous foe.

"Hello, Charlie-O," said the Queen, her shark teeth gleaming in a wicked grin. How Charlie despised her! He wanted to spit in her eyes, but she had six of the things, and they were well out of his reach.

The Queen then lifted her hand and breathed across it, just as she had done the first time they met. But Charlie knew the truth of her now. The power of her name alone had no effect on him.

"I'm not afraid of you," he boldly declared.

"Oh?" said the Queen. "But you wear your fear so plainly! I can see it without even looking at you. You're afraid of everything, Charlie Oughtt, and I'm ten thousand times more frightening than all the things that keep you awake in the night. Give up, child. You cannot win against me. Submit your memory to me, and you will never know pain again."

Do it! Do it now, while her eyes are looking the other way! Charlie screamed in his head. "The only world I'm building for you is your prison!" he shouted as he bolted for that pale monarch of horror, brandishing the key like a blade aimed straight for her evil heart. But the Queen's head quite unexpectedly swiveled around until her red gaze bore furiously into him. Her body soon followed her head, and she charged backward at her boy opponent, her arms popping and clicking out of joint so that they could reach for him.

Squeezing the key tightly, Charlie ran from the Queen, but the Queen pressed on. From her open palms a thousand bedbugs poured, trickling between her fingers and dropping to the floor, where they raced for him in a deadly stream. Charlie imagined sharp spikes all over them, and the insects squealed as their shells distorted. They were stuck to the floor and to each other, and some were buried deep into the Queen's skin like burrs. The Queen screamed and stopped in her tracks, cradling her wounded hands in front of her.

"I must compliment you on your quick learning," she said, sucking air between her tiny teeth in her pain. The thunder had gone out of her voice and agony distorted her face. "But you will never be a match for the mistress of all fear, and that is a lesson *you will now be taught.*"

The Queen didn't take a single step. As swiftly as a thought, the place beneath her feet turned to ice, and the ice spread across the whole floor. Charlie wasn't fast enough to think of a defense, and the moment he moved, he slipped, landing with embarrassment on his backside. But he did not drop the key. He kept it buried so deeply in his hand that blood dripped from his fist, and the blood made scarlet coins where it froze upon the frigid floor.

As Charlie rose to his feet all wobbly and unsure, the Queen was growing into something else entirely. Her neck stretched up, up, up to the ceiling while her gown grew rounder, wider, longer until it had turned into a serpent's tail. Then her arms shrank into her body until there weren't any arms at all, and where once she had only one long neck, now she had seven even longer ones. Each of these bore copies of her eyeless face, and out of every head spiraled a pair of curly black horns. No longer was the Queen some distorted picture of a Tudor noble. Now Charlie stood before a towering hydra.

"What?" he gasped—all he had time to think before each of the hydra heads spewed cold blue bolts of frozen fire in his direction. If Charlie hadn't ducked in time, he would have been pierced through the middle by them. The Queen drew each of her heads back to spit out another round of arctic flame, but this time Charlie was prepared.

"Don't you doubt yourself. Don't you dare!" he shouted to himself, and he stood straight as an arrow, eyeing those piercing ice bolts straight on. With all of his concentration he fought, until at

last the frozen flames stopped mere inches from his nose. Then he willed them to turn around and fly right back for the heads that had breathed them.

The Queen, however, was just as prepared as Charlie. Soon, her whole body glowed bright orange as her heads drew back again to breathe not ice but true fire. Again Charlie ducked, but he had not been her target this time. It was her own frozen plumes she sought to consume, instantly reducing them to steam. Now the air was thick with fog, and Charlie found himself lost in a world of white.

"Only an infant would make such a foolish mistake!" hissed the Queen. He could hear her, but he could not see her.

"I think now that I was wrong about you," she said from somewhere else in the fog. "You could never be a builder of worlds. You have no true gift. You're merely a weed that keeps growing back. And weeds should be torn out by their roots."

Charlie felt a tickle around his ankles, only the fog was still too thick to see what caused the sensation. The tickling crept over his shins and then spread to his knees. He tried to move away, but something gripped his legs and held on fiercely. It was moving up now, stretching past his knees. The tickling became pain as barbed vines gripped his skin all over. Charlie reached down to pull the barbs away yet managed only to cut his fingers.

He wanted to stop the vines, to will them into slowing their growth, but the Queen's power over them was too great. For all of Charlie's concentration, they climbed on and on. Now they wrapped around his middle and stretched up over his ribs. He cried out in panic and in response heard tiny screams, mimicking him.

"What is this?" he shouted. As the vines grew nearer to his face, he could finally see them, hazy in the mist. They were as black as the Queen's gown, and sprouting from the vines were small white buds. Buds with faces that copied his own but without any eyes, imitating his every expression.

Charlie fought to pull them off despite the pain. They gripped like the devil, though, twisting around his arms and shoulders.

"I feel this is meant to be symbolic or something!" he shouted, laughing just to keep his courage up. "If it's all right with you, I'd rather get straight to the point!"

He glared at the floor, and though he could not see the checkerboard squares, he knew they were there. Then he thought with all his might until one of them broke into sharp pieces. Soon, the shards were hacking away with unseen hands, sawing at the vines until they dropped off, screeching horribly.

"Ha!" Charlie jeered as he pulled the last of the thorns from his ankles. "For someone made out of thoughts, you aren't very creative, are you?"

"For a serious boy with a sister in his care, you certainly are *careless*," seethed the Queen in reply. Her fingertips had turned as black as ink, and that ink was traveling up her veins. Strange bumps formed all over her arms now, and the bumps turned into slimy little suckers. And then, as soon as Charlie blinked, the Queen's appendages were long, stretchy tentacles. Now she had eight of them. Her skin, her dress, and everything about her had become slick and rubbery, and she was positively enormous.

She's turned herself into a kraken! Charlie thought. *How in the world am I supposed to fight a kraken?*

There was no time to react before the Queen lashed at Charlie with one of her massive tentacles. He tried to dodge but he wasn't quick enough, and he soon found himself wrapped from ankle to throat in a hold that was sure to strangle him. With the tip of another slippery arm, the Queen pried at his hand, determined to wrest the key away. Charlie would not let go. His head felt light, and he had begun to see stars before his eyes. Still, he refused to give up so easily. He wished dearly that he could find anything else to use as a weapon. His imaginative powers were fading along with his ability to breathe, though, and all he could see from where he struggled were statues in pieces.

Hold on. That's it! thought Charlie just as his vision was starting to blur.

They had been there the whole time, those broken chunks of marble, almost as if they were waiting to be used. *Move, you knocked-off heads and broken arms! Fly through the room, you limbless torsos! Come this way! Come this way and pin down all the Queen's arms!*

It was the simplest of anything Charlie had thought up yet, but it was just about the only thing he *could* think of. The Queen was so intent upon stealing the key that she had abandoned all thought of the items within her own chamber. How she roared as those carved pieces soared through the air and slammed down upon all her free arms! Those arms that had taunted Charlie released him at once, and he collapsed to the floor, gasping for air, the key still safely in his bleeding hand.

It would be the Queen's move next, and Charlie couldn't simply stand aside and wait for her attack. He had to strike while his nemesis remained distracted, and she was bound to recover quickly.

Charlie focused his attention on the filigree brooch, which looked minuscule against her mighty kraken form. He thought that if he could only climb across one of her arms while it remained pinned, then he could drive the key into her heart and begin the final battle for her destruction.

Charlie wasted no further time thinking and raced up her arm even as the Queen hissed and screamed and thrashed beneath the weight. He was so very close. It could have been easy to pop the key in and give it a turn.

But it wasn't to be such a simple task. Somewhere in his mind, Charlie had known it wouldn't be, yet he had, for just a moment, hoped. The Queen had tricked him with all that tortured wailing. She had waited for exactly this moment to regain her true form, sending Charlie plummeting to the floor. He landed flat on his back. Pain raced all through his body, from his spine to the tips of his fingers, and the wind flew out of him. Try as he might, he couldn't recover as rapidly as the Queen. Alas, he was only human.

Fast, faster than Charlie could blink, the Queen whirled around, and her ten fingers separated from her hands, sharp as knives and speeding directly for Charlie's chest.

"Ack!" he sputtered, and in a panic, he turned to the only object he had handy—the key. Before he realized what he was thinking, the key flattened out and spread until it had taken the shape of a golden shield. *Thunk! Thunk! Thunk-thunk-thunk!* went the ten blades that had once been the Queen's own fingers as they buried themselves into the surface of Charlie's shield.

"Oh no!" Charlie cried. *What've I done?* he thought. For he had turned his only weapon of real value into something else completely, and he would never be able to remember the key exactly the way it had been before. How would he unlock the Queen now?

"I've ruined it," he groaned. "I've ruined everything forever!"

The shield felt so heavy now, and its weight increased as the seconds ticked by. Charlie peered out from under an edge and saw the Queen gliding toward him, muttering strange incantations. *She's controlling it!* Charlie thought. *First I ruined the key, and now she's using it against me!*

Charlie lay helplessly beneath the increasingly heavy weight, unable to move, unable to throw it off himself. Meanwhile, the Queen swiftly approached.

"You will die now, and I will not even honor you," she thundered. "A shame. You could have ruled an entire world."

Charlie watched in mortal dread as the Queen's arms thinned and sharpened. The stubs of each fingerless hand grew and fused into a single point until both her arms were ivory blades. She threw herself down and dragged herself to Charlie by her sword arms, each one clanking fiercely as it met the floor, sparks flying. It was sheer horror to see her; she crawled so impossibly fast. With a war cry, she reached her prize and raised her diabolical blades to plunge them into Charlie's chest and end him forevermore. He knew his shield would be useless against her.

Charlie acted at once. He would never know how he thought so quickly, but it was with remarkable speed that the unbearably heavy shield became a sword itself. It was thin and light but ever so sharp. Without delay, Charlie drove the sword into the evil queen's chest just as her own blade arrived inches from his heart.

The Queen stopped at once. As if pulled up on a string, she stood again. Then she twisted her head around to observe the damage done. Charlie was nearly as surprised as she. *I . . . I didn't ruin it,* he thought. The sword he'd shaped out of the shield—the shield that was once the key—had become the key again, fitted perfectly into the Queen's lock. Her six red eyes regarded it with what appeared to be fear at first and then, or so it seemed, with mirth. Her head swiveled the right way around, the blades at her shoulders twisted back into arms and hands, and her terrible mouth grinned as beetles streamed like blood through her little shark teeth, spilling lifelessly down her chin.

Charlie felt an unbearable chill as he watched this new terror reveal itself to him. The key turned on its own with a *click.* Then a seam formed at the place where the keyhole was affixed, and it spread up and down through the middle of the Queen's body. All the while, she smiled, and her chest shook with silent laughter. Slowly, her split body opened up like a steamer trunk, and—*whoosh!*—out from within her flew a cold black wind. It bathed the royal chamber in darkness so grave that even Charlie's soul felt cold.

Charlie stood in the pure black darkness, his blood pounding in his ears. The true battle, against the painful memory that had failed all other rememberers before him, was beginning. But he *knew* he would win. There was simply no possibility that Charlie could be broken now, he told himself. No, not by that. Nevertheless, he closed his eyes and feared to open them again.

Open them he did, however, and upon doing so found himself in the first house he had ever known. It was just as he had expected. This was when he would be awakened. This was when the terrible

news would be delivered. When Mother would cry, and the man at the door would stand there awkwardly, hat in hands.

And yet something was wrong. Charlie wasn't lying in his bed, for starters. Rather, he sat in the old dining room before a table laden with little presents and a cake that glowed with six small candles. He heard his mother playing a happy song on the piano in another room. Georgie, so small here, sat at the end of the dining table, trying to crawl up onto it. She was only two.

Dread struck Charlie down as cleanly as a brand-new hatchet. This was not the memory he had expected. No, it was far, far worse. Because it was not the night that Father died. No, it was instead the evening of Charlie's sixth birthday—the happiest memory he had of Father. And because it was the happiest—because he would never have another like it—it pained him the most to think of it. For that reason, he had refused to think of it at all for six long years.

"You've won," he whispered as hot tears welled up in his eyes. "You've beaten me."

Charlie's sight blurred as the tears broke free of their prison and trickled down his cheeks. For years he hadn't successfully cried a single drop, and now he couldn't keep the tears inside. *It shouldn't have been this memory,* Charlie thought. *How could anyone be so unkind?*

Mother stopped playing the piano and clapped her hands gleefully as the front door opened. In stepped Father from the snow, carrying a small box wrapped in brown paper.

"I've had this hidden in the shed for quite a while, my boy, and I nearly thought I'd lost it!" said Father as he placed the package on the table with the others.

"Please don't," said Charlie. "I don't want it. Not now."

But Father didn't hear him. He just kept cheerfully on. "You've such a knack for sniffing out all my hiding places, I had to be extra careful this time! We ought to call you Sherlock Holmes."

"Now, now. Don't tease him on his big day," Mother playfully scolded Father. "Let him open his presents!"

"I don't want to open anything. Please, everyone. Just go away," Charlie said. Again, no one seemed to hear or see him. They were speaking to the happy six-year-old he used to be. Not the frightened, heartbroken twelve-year-old he was now.

Georgie—that is, little two-year-old Georgie—crawled across the tabletop and took hold of a smaller present. It would be a little windup monkey made of tin, Charlie remembered, but it would never work right because Georgie had dropped it from the table that day and bent the key so that it wouldn't turn anymore.

"Oh no, Georgie!" Mother cried out, and she rushed to swoop up Charlie's sister. Just as it happened long ago, Georgie dropped the little package, and it landed on the floor with a crunch. While Mother was preoccupied with Charlie's sister, Father nudged the paper-wrapped box toward him.

"Go ahead. Before your little sister can get ahold of it," said Father.

"I can't," said Charlie, wiping his dripping nose on his sleeve, but something compelled him to open the gift all the same. Of course, it would be his old alarm clock. The one that would faithfully signal the same hour for over two thousand more days before *the grandmothers*. A day without it never felt right, and yet he had never allowed himself to think about the day he received it.

"This was my bedside clock until I married your mother," said Father. "I know it isn't much fun for a gift, but, well, I wanted you to know that I think you're growing into a smart young man. And a smart young man needs the right tools to start his day. How do you like it?"

"It's the best present I've ever gotten," Charlie whispered. It was exactly what he had said at the time, but of course, his heart hadn't been breaking into a thousand pieces then. At the time, he had been beaming with pride because he was going to be just like Father.

"I've had your name engraved on the back. I wasn't sure if Mother would be able to keep the secret!" Father said with a warm smile.

The cuckoo clock in the hall chirped its evening call six times, and Father pulled out his pocket watch. "I hate to leave you, my boy, but I'm afraid I have to go in to the mill tonight," he said.

After ruffling Charlie's hair, he added, "Someday you'll be managing that mill yourself! Won't be long before you don't need your old man at all."

"I'll always need you!" Charlie cried, and he could no longer contain his grief. The chains that had held his heart together for so long had finally broken, and Charlie sobbed without hesitation.

But Father didn't hear him. He just smiled, grabbed his hat from the hall tree, and walked out the door. Father would return later, and there would be days of mundane life that younger Charlie wouldn't appreciate just yet.

Then one night, Father would go off to work, and he wouldn't come home again.

"Please come back," Charlie whispered. He buried his head in his arms and wept.

Of all the times for his heart chains to break! Now when he needed them the most! So distraught had Charlie become that he did not care that the room was growing colder and the light dimmer. He didn't see that a shadow was stretching over his feet in the shape of his cruelest foe. Had he glanced up but once, he would have witnessed the Queen rising, dragging her still-forming body across a checkered floor to him, one hand—not quite solid yet—before the other, vicious intention gleaming from her beetle-flecked smile.

"*You slept that night. The night the terrible thing happened,*" said a wicked whisper that sounded a lot like the Queen.

"I didn't know," Charlie cried into his arms.

"*Your world was breaking apart, and yet you dreamed peacefully in comfort,*" the whisper went on. "*Is that why you no longer sleep, Charlie Oughtt? Is that why you hate to dream?*"

"Say whatever you want. I don't care anymore," Charlie cried, though it was a painful lie. In truth, the Queen's words cut him more deeply than her sword arms and finger knives ever could have. Charlie felt like he was shrinking inside himself, that he was a very small creature within a larger shell that would surely break apart and land hopelessly on the ground quite soon if no one helped him, and he was sure that no one could.

But help *did* come.

It came in the form of an earsplitting sound—the unrelenting peal of copper bells just like the ones that used to sound off Charlie's every morning before the grandmothers took them away. Charlie looked up slowly, confused, and saw that the dream of his birthday had cleared away. Gone was the dining room, the table decked with presents. He stood again in the middle of the throne room. In front of him, the pale queen writhed on her knees, her hands to her ears, teeth clenched in pain.

"Time to wake up, Charlie-O!" someone announced behind him.

"Georgie?" Charlie said. He dried his eyes and turned warily, afraid it would be another trick. But there stood his sister, safe and sound, holding his beloved alarm clock over her head.

"Georgie . . . ," he murmured. *Yes, Georgie,* he thought. *Georgie's still alive. Father's gone, but Georgie's not! And with any luck, Mother's safe at home. I haven't lost everything! Father would want me to remember that. He wouldn't want me to spend so much time grieving that I forget to be happy. That I forget how much I still have. . . .*

"Georgie!" he shouted, shaking off the effect of the dream. Georgie ran to him and threw her arms around him, laughing. The alarm clock rattled on.

"You remember me!" said Charlie.

"Of course I remember you, big brother!" said Georgie, pulling away. Charlie noticed she looked a little older than the last time he'd seen her.

"I think I always remembered," she said. "It was only buried somewhere. Just like your clock! I found it that day in the hammering hall, and I *knew* it was familiar, but I didn't know why! So, I hid it, hoping it would all come back to me. And it did, Charlie! Your friends came in and smashed up the figment chamber with their hammers, and suddenly I could remember! What a riot it was, too. You should have seen everyone hacking away at the roots with their hammers like . . . like warriors!"

"You must promise to tell me all about it when we get out of here,"

Charlie gently interrupted her. He glanced back nervously at the struggling queen. "Where are the other children now?"

"They've all gone above. I came back to find you, and I didn't see anyone left," said Georgie.

"Good," said Charlie. "We should get going ourselves. But first I have some business to finish. Keep back."

Georgie nodded and clutched the alarm clock close. Somehow, the little hammer between its bells kept clanging away as if by magic, though it ought to have long since run down. Perhaps it *was* magic. There were mysteries yet to be solved in this dark cave, mysteries that might very well remain unsolved until the end of time. For now, Charlie had the Queen to deal with.

The Queen thrashed on the floor, howling with rage and from the pain of an interrupted reemergence. She had been so close, so very close to regaining her physical form. But her link with Charlie's pain had been broken too soon. A fine web of cracks spread all through her skin, and there was a black hole over her heart, framed with rot, where once there had been a place for a key.

Charlie stood over her, all fear he had ever felt for her lost. "You really thought you could take the world for yourself, didn't you?" he said to her. "You thought we kids would do all the work for you, too, if you frightened us enough. But you were wrong. We're stronger than that."

The Queen swatted blindly at him and missed. "You're weak ... weak. . . . You would have . . . given up . . . if your little sister . . . hadn't come to your . . . rescue . . . ," she spat.

Charlie shook his head. "You'll never understand," he said. "I'm stronger than you could ever be because I have people to love, people who love *me*. I forgot what that meant for a while. I was always so scared of losing them that it was all I thought about. But I *haven't* lost them. That's what I needed to remember. There's so much more to life than being afraid of loss, and I'm never going to let fear stop me from living again."

The Queen groaned and wrapped her arms around her middle. She was withering away now. With every word Charlie spoke to her, she lessened a little bit more. "Mercy! Mercy!" she pleaded, her voice, once thunderous, now nothing greater than a gentle evening breeze.

"Go back to where you belong and leave us be," said Charlie. "We aren't frightened of you anymore."

"I will torment you . . . in your dreams . . . forever . . . ," the Queen wheezed.

And then the Queen was no more. She disintegrated into dust, and that, too, was quickly blown away. The Queen of fear was not dead, no, but drawn back into the realm of the imaginary into which she had been born. In the distance, Charlie heard the phantoms howl with joy, a howl that was abruptly silenced. The phantoms, too, had gone home at last.

"What happened to the Queen?" Georgie asked.

"She lost," was all Charlie said.

The throne room gave a violent tremble, showering Charlie and Georgie in a torrent of dirt and small rocks.

"It's because the harvest trees are dying," Georgie said. "I watched one wilting when I went up into the house. Oh, Charlie! We'll be trapped forever if we don't get out in time!"

"Then we'd better run, hadn't we?" said Charlie.

"I'm not ashamed to admit that I'm terribly frightened!" said Georgie.

Charlie grinned and took his sister's hand. "Think of it as an adventure!" he said.

Charlie and Georgie ran as fast as either had ever done, which was saying quite a lot in Georgie's case. It seemed a hundred years before they reached the great hall, and the journey wasn't an easy one. As the living nightmare died, tunnels collapsed, the walls caved in, and structures broke down into dust. What tunnels there were that remained standing tried their best to change course in a desperate final attempt to keep the Oughtt children from escaping. But through Charlie's skills, Georgie's resourcefulness, and a few last miracles, they made it into the great hall just as the entrance crumbled behind them. Now there was only one tunnel left to travel. But with all the crashing and smashing of the end of this nightmare world, it was going to be the hardest tunnel yet.

CHAPTER THIRTEEN

CHARLIE AND GEORGIE AND MOTHER

Fast, faster, and even faster the children ran. Their lungs hurt and they had stitches in their sides, but they could not stop or they would surely be trapped forever. Yet every time it seemed they were gaining ground, the road ahead of them grew even longer.

"Where's the confounded exit?" Charlie asked.

"I don't know! I don't remember this tunnel being so long before!" Georgie cried.

Behind them, the walls caved in, groaning as if in pain. Once, Charlie tried to slow their collapse, but he could manage to move only a few fragments of rock now. *The magic is dying, too,* he thought.

"Look! Up ahead!" said Georgie, pointing. For just before them, projected on the wall, was a human silhouette.

"Hey!" said this shadow in a familiar voice. "This way, you two! And hurry!"

As if there was any other way to go! But the children were glad to hear a human being all the same.

"Thank goodness! It's Badger Brush!" Charlie breathed with relief. "Are you lost, too?"

"No, silly!" answered Badger Brush. "I just came back for you, is all. We're really not far from the opening, but we don't have much time. The ladder up is starting to get goopy. My name's Mateus, by the way. I'm starting to remember again! And just when 'Badger Brush' was growing on me. Anyway, come on! Follow me!"

"Pleased to meet you, Mateus," said Georgie, and the three children ran on until they came to the steps they had each descended once before. It was as dark as ever, even with the torch that Badger Brush, now Mateus, held.

Mateus lifted that feeble torch and pointed the way ahead. In the dim light, Charlie saw that his friend's shoulder was bleeding from a fearsome gash.

"What *happened* to you?" Charlie asked.

"Oh. That," said Mateus with a shrug that made him wince. "Just a rumble with one of the last sandmen. He was guarding the harvest tree up there. The way everything's falling apart, I figure it's the only one still alive, and *golly*, he sure was bent on saving it!"

"What happened after that?" asked Georgie.

"The tree fell down on its own," said Mateus. "Now Mister Sandman's just a pile of sand underneath it. Oh, here's the ladder!"

The three climbed the ladder as quickly as they could, but it was difficult, for the ladder was elastic now and terribly sticky, too. Its rungs drooped and clung like stretched-out chewing gum. It got

216

worse the longer they climbed, and sometimes it seemed they'd never reach the top before the whole ladder was nothing but strings.

"We're not going to make it!" Georgie cried.

"Yes, we will! Keep looking up!" Charlie urged her. "But quickly, please. Quickly!"

"We're trying!" Georgie screamed back, struggling to free her feet from a melting rung.

And then there was light. Mateus reached the opening to the tunnel and, with no small amount of effort, managed to push open the cellar door. Each child stumbled out into the strange world above, gulping the fresh air. Charlie was the last to exit, and he shouted with joy as he slammed the cellar door closed forever.

Though the sky was still very dark from the storm clouds, there was at least light enough to tell it wasn't night anymore. The sunlight, clouded as it was, hurt the children's eyes. But the sight they saw when they recovered was like nothing they could have imagined.

The farmhouse was all but gone. The cellar door through which they had just leaped hovered in its familiar place while attached to absolutely nothing. The house itself remained little more than a rapidly rotting frame, and in the midst of that frame teetered a tower of forgotten toys and belongings that reached the sky, disappearing into the clouds. It was much taller than the heaps of toys Charlie had found when he stumbled across that forbidden room what seemed like so long ago, but he knew it was the same. The farmhouse and its strange dimension were fading away, like the grandmothers who had once operated it. Reality was forcing its way in again.

As for the farm, it was merely a dry desert bed now. Even the snow was gone. Thousands of free children wandered its cracked surface,

many clutching belongings they'd found in the pile. To Charlie, it looked like an ocean of gray uniforms and bewilderment.

Mateus said something then and pointed ahead. He seemed surprised, but Charlie could not understand a word he said.

"*Olhe para a árvore!*" Mateus repeated.

And then Charlie understood what was happening. *Of course,* he thought with a little sadness. *Why did I never think of that before?* Down in the nightmare caves, everyone spoke the same language. Or if they did not speak it, they heard it just as if they did. But now the magic was dying, and with it, that same gift that made so many friends even in the midst of their troubles. Now each child spoke his own tongue.

"I think he means the harvest tree," said Georgie. "It's nearly dead. Look what it's become!"

Just as she said, the harvest tree, once an upright if leafless elm, lay across the desert floor as a series of lazy limbs draped along the parched ground. There must have been scores of others just like it all around the world. Its ropelike limbs pulsed weakly, but they wilted more the longer Charlie watched.

"What do we do now?" he asked quietly.

"I suppose we must walk until we find someone to help us," said Georgie.

"*Eu não faço idéia do que você acabou de falar,*" said Mateus with a sad sigh.

Just then, the long ropes of the harvest tree's dying branches withdrew into the earth, and there was a mighty quaking. The multitudes of children screamed and clung to one another fearfully. Deep fissures formed throughout the ground. *The whole land looks like the Queen did before the end,* thought Charlie.

It was his last thought before a great chasm opened up and all the ground beneath their feet was simply . . . gone.

There was darkness. In the darkness there was nothing but a sensation of falling. No sound save for the wind whooshing past their ears. That was all Georgie and Charlie knew as they clung to one another, waiting fearfully for the bottom.

But if there *was* a bottom to this seemingly bottomless pit, Charlie and Georgie must have awoken before they landed. For there they were, both sitting up in their own beds in their old bedroom at home, as if they had never left it at all. The children sprang up to pull back the dividing curtain. Charlie laughed, but Georgie frowned.

"What's wrong?" Charlie asked. "We're home! At least, it looks like home."

"It wasn't a dream, was it?" asked Georgie. "Because it looks to *me* like we woke up from a long sleep. Like everything we just did, the adventures we just had, were only a dream. And oh, how I *loathe* stories that end that way!"

"We can't both have had the same nightmare," Charlie pointed out. "And look! We're still wearing our uniforms!"

Georgie looked at her brother and then examined her own clothing, the same old ugly grays.

"I *knew* it was real," she whispered with a smile, but then she looked worried. "How do we know it's over?"

It was a very good question. The Queen's ability to manifest her creations was frightening. The children had watched her shrivel away, but how could they be sure it really happened and wasn't simply another twisted trick?

"I've got an idea," said Charlie.

He stared at the drawn curtain. He stared at it long and hard.

"What are you trying to—" Georgie began.

"Shh!" Charlie interrupted her.

Billow like a ship's sail! he commanded with his thoughts. But the curtain simply hung there on its rod, lifeless and dull. Charlie was glad of it, but in some way, he was also a little sad. The magic was gone, and he was only an ordinary boy again.

"Looks to me like it's over," he said, and then, "but what about Mother?"

"Oh!" Georgie squeaked. "We must go to her at once! What if she isn't even here?"

The children sprinted to Mother's bedroom double-quick. There they found her in her bed, fast asleep, but not at all peacefully. She tossed and turned and turned and tossed, feverishly murmuring their names.

"Mama," Georgie whispered, gently shaking her. "Mama, wake up."

Mother cried out and bolted upright in bed. "Georgie? Charlie?" she gasped once she had recovered. "What are you both doing out of bed? And what are these rags you're both wearing? Are you all right?"

"Well, yes, Mama, but . . . ," Georgie began.

"We, er . . . ," Charlie struggled.

"Oh, it doesn't matter. Come here, darlings," said Mother, getting up to hug her children close. She said, "I had the most terrible nightmare about the both of you! I sent you away to some horrible old crones, but I couldn't remember why I did it, and—"

The children consoled their mother, and when the consoling was done, Charlie found that he could see starlight through Mother's window. It had been a long time since the clouds allowed the stars to shine so brightly.

"Let's go sit on the porch steps and look at the moon, Mother," said Charlie.

"Oh yes! That would be wonderful!" Georgie agreed.

Mother was mystified. "But, Charlie! It's so cold out there! Aren't you worried you'll catch your death?"

"We have coats, haven't we?" said Charlie. "Really, Mother, you shouldn't worry so."

Georgie giggled. Mother frowned and felt Charlie's forehead but eventually shook her head and took her young ones outside to see the first clear night in ages. The Oughtt children each wondered, silently, what had become of the neighbor children. If they found similar ends to their nightmares. If they would ever speak to one another about those strange, horrible days in the caves. And what of Badger Brush, Milkweed, and all their other friends? What of the poor rag-and-bone woman? These were all questions for another time. For now, it felt right just to be home, to be safe, and to be loved.

That night, Charlie slept, and in his dreams, Father sat at his bedside. They talked awhile about Mother and Georgie until a shiny black beetle the size of Charlie's thumb crawled up his arm. It hissed at him and snapped its pincers. But then Father simply reached over and brushed the little thing aside, and the two of them sang songs while the beetle flew out the open window and away.

It wasn't until nearly ten the next morning that Charlie awoke. And when he did, it was with a smile on his face and a wonderful feeling of excitement about the day ahead.

ABOUT THE AUTHOR

KATY TOWELL was, by most accounts, an exemplary student and a well-behaved child back in Kansas. Her parents do not know where they went wrong. Today, Ms. Towell is a graphic designer, writer, and illustrator in Portland, Oregon, with dreams of one day being the scary old lady in the house about which all the neighborhood children tell ghost stories. She is the writer, illustrator, and sometimes animator of the website Childrin R Skary. In her spare time, Ms. Towell collects antiques, strange teas, and carnivorous houseplants, and she plays a little tune on her violin now and again. Learn more at skary.com.

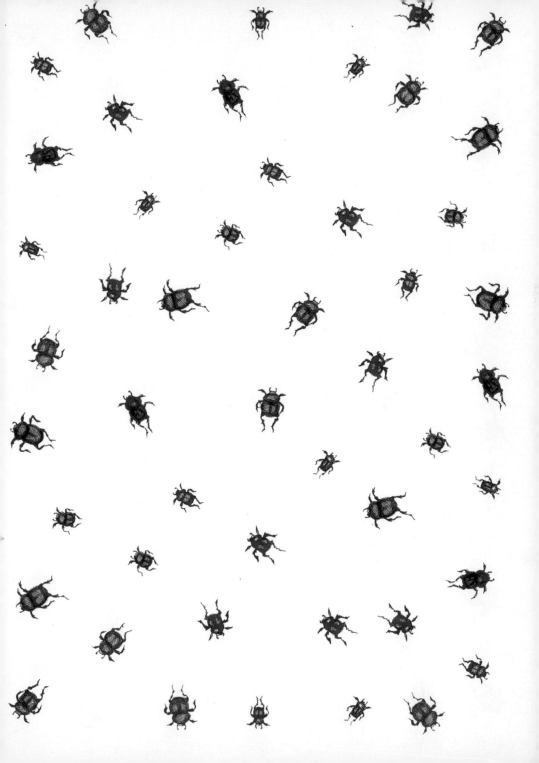

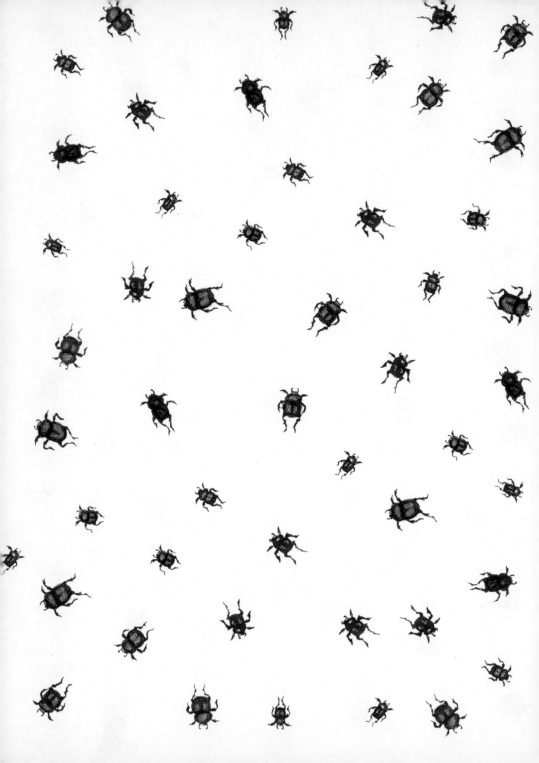

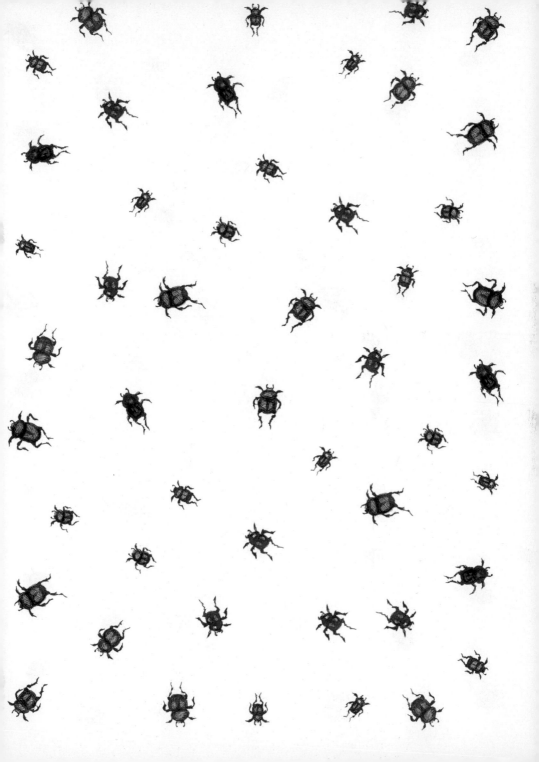

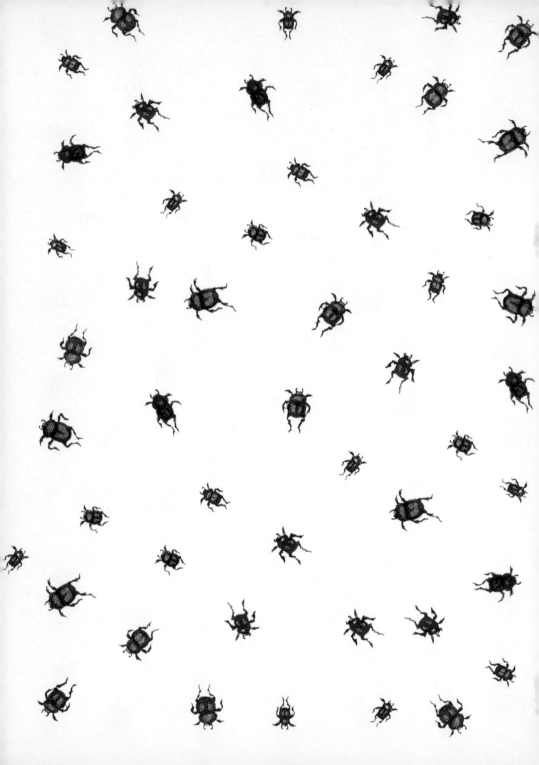